WHO REALLY CARES?

HELEN OVBIAGELE

DEDICATION

For my family: **Bruce Snr.; Bruce Jnr.; Desmond; Ohifemen; Ojekhoa; Adesuwa;**

and my friend **Stella Kragha**, *for their* support and encouragement.

CONTENTS

CHAPTER 1

The two men sat on their beds and looked solemnly at each other as they thought of their imminent parting. They had been cell-mates at the **Sabo Prison** in **Onitsha** for four years and had become good friends.

Diba Anang, alias '**Andy Brown**', broke the silence. "What will become of me? What will I do and where will I go to?" he asked dejectedly.

"Stop behaving like a woman," said **Sunu Matte**, alias '**Flint**' and a dozen other names. "You'll do what others before you have done when they left prison. You'll rebuild your life."

"What life? After ten years in jail? I'm almost afraid to leave this place where I feel so safe and secure."

"Safe and secure!" exclaimed the other

man scornfully. "In jail! You must be out of your mind. Out there," he went on, nodding in the direction of the prison gates, "there's a world of **freedom and opportunity** waiting for you. A place where you can show people what you're worth and capable of. Man! What wouldn't I give to be in your shoes and know that tomorrow I would leave this hole and would be a free citizen again, and continue with my rightful existence. Wow!"

He jumped up and slammed a fist into his palm. He sat down again quickly when a passing warden told him to shut up. Long ago, Flint would have rained abuse on the man and later made sure he was beaten up when he took inmates out to work in the field, but he had since learnt that this prison wing was **different from all the others**. The guards were very tough. Apart from their impressive physical appearance, they could kill with their bare hands without leaving any tell-tale marks on their victims. He often wondered where they were trained. He still ached all over whenever he remembered the beating he had received from one of them his first time there. He had seen the most fearful criminal in that maximum security wing beaten and hounded by these guards until the man had finally taken his own life in order to be at peace. By appearing docile and by being co-operative Flint had been able to steer clear of trouble and had even made a few friends amongst the guards.

"See," he continued in a low voice when the guard was out of sight, "I've a plan for whenever I get out of here, and that should be quite soon. It's a **master plan that's foolproof.** I've already contacted people here and outside. They are on the alert and this time we're going to pull off something big, really big, and no one is going to get me inside again. After that, I'll retire from the profession a very rich man and spend the rest of my life in a remote corner of the country or emigrate to one of the neighbouring countries. I might even marry and raise children..."

As he listened, Diba doubted if Flint would ever retire from his chosen career, nor could he see him withdrawing to the remote corner of anywhere, for the man was an **extrovert** who thoroughly enjoyed his criminal activities. Although they were good friends, they came from very different backgrounds.

Flint, who was now in his late forties, was a good-looking, thickset man of average height with a **devil-may-care attitude** which won him admiration everywhere, even from his enemies. He appeared tough, and was—physically and emotionally.

A flood which had swept through his village had made him a homeless orphan at the age of eight. He had been the only survivor in his family and had been picked up along with other orphans by voluntary workers and taken to a large camp. He hated the camp intensely. There had been swarms of sad-looking children everywhere being herded about by totally indifferent welfare workers. Everything had been so impersonal. No one had actually cared one way or the other what happened to the children. Many had died and several, including Flint, had run away. He had always been sharp and at an early age had been given the responsibility of looking after younger children. When he left the camp, he had trekked to a neighbouring village where his maternal grandparents lived and had been horrified to find it in ruins. Everything had been swept away by floods. He finally understood why no one had come to look for him at the camp. His family had been wiped out! Feeling alone in the world and frightened as he looked at the ruins, he had sat down on a fallen tree and wept. Some villagers had been searching among the debris to see if anything could be salvaged and others were busy burying corpses so as to prevent an epidemic. Nobody had paid him any attention. Stray children were a common sight and anyway, everyone had his troubles. Hunger had soon made him shake himself out of his self-pity and he had begun to wonder how he was going to feed himself.

He had trekked from village to village begging for food and had finally become a **'motor boy'** in **Owerri**. He worked in **Aba,**

Enugu and **Onitsha** until he was about thirteen when he took to picking pockets at motor parks and in market places. He had not been forced into it; he had simply decided that stealing was a better and an easier way of earning quick money to satisfy the taste for expensive things and fast living which he had acquired. He needed a lot of money for this, so graduating from being a petty thief to being a **hardened armed robber** was for him a natural step. He wanted the best for himself and he did not mind how he came about it. He felt he owed society nothing; after all, society had done nothing for him. As a teenager, he had been sent to jail in various parts of the country. He felt no qualms about his nefarious activities and he always told himself that, if he had to live his life all over again, he would not change a single thing—except perhaps he might have started a criminal life earlier.

Diba, on the other hand, had been brought up in a **religious, middle-class family** where members went about preaching the word of God every weekend.

His father was an elder in his religious
organisation and was highly respected in
Ukum, a large village not far from **Uyo** in
the **Cross River State**. Diba was the fourth
of the six children in the family and at the
age of sixteen he had got his 'O' levels. He
was an intelligent boy and his parents ought
to have been proud of him but they were
not. In fact, he was considered a disgrace to
their respectable family because of his
pilfering. This had started at an early age
and at first it had been dismissed as a
passing phase, but when it continued into
his teenage years the family had become
worried. Help had been sought from all
sources. Prayers had been said for him,
native and medical doctors had been
consulted, but to no avail. The principal of
his school and the doctor had called it
'kleptomania' and had said he might drop
the habit later, but everyone else believed
that he would always remain a thief. He had
brought dishonour to the family and should
be done away with, for how could the other
members go about asking people to repent
from their sinful ways when one of them
could not keep his fingers off other people's

things? It was most embarrassing. Diba was the most tormented by his handicap. He could not control his **itching fingers**. Many of the things he took he had to throw away as he really had no use for them. At times he did not even realise he had picked them up. He had felt very humiliated while at boarding school when missing articles had been traced to him. He had felt an outcast but he had not been dismissed because of his brilliant academic performance. When he left school, his father decided to send him away, the further away the better. He was therefore sent to his **Uncle Ewah** in **Lagos**. Ewah had left home in his teens to seek his fortune in the big city; he rarely visited Ukum and so he knew nothing about Diba's handicap. He was married with three children and he worked as a cook for **Chief Laja**, a wealthy business-man who lived in an exclusive area in **Apapa**. He and his wife were glad to have a young person around the house now that their children were away at school.

Diba was a pleasant boy and he sometimes went to the Chief's kitchen to help his uncle. For a while things went on well, then Ewah found some items from the Laja household in his own house. He was horrified to discover that his handsome and educated nephew was a thief. Perhaps the boy had been tempted by all the nice things lying around? Ewah spoke to Diba kindly and advised him to put a stop to the habit. When it continued he threatened to send him away; meanwhile he stopped him from coming over to the big house. He did not want any disgrace. He had served the Laja family for over ten years and neither he nor any member of his family had ever been accused of theft. After several letters on the issue to his brother, he got a reply saying that he could send the boy away if he liked but Diba was not exactly welcome back home. This saddened Ewah as he liked Diba and felt that the boy needed help. He did not think that sending him cold-heartedly away would solve the problem so he tried to think of what he could do to set things right.

But matters got worse when **Toki**, Chief Laja's fifteen-year-old daughter, who was in her fourth year at a local grammar school, became pregnant and said that **Diba was responsible for her condition**.

Everybody trembled as Chief Laja exploded into a rage at the news. Until then, he and his wife had counted themselves lucky that their youngest daughter had given them no teenage headaches whatsoever, as she had time for little else besides her studies. She took absolutely no interest in boys or parties and had very few girlfriends. She must have been led astray by the cook's nephew.

After giving the matter much thought, however, the Chief calmed down and decided not to fire Ewah who had given such a long and loyal service. Besides, good cooks like him were hard to come by. The man was not responsible for his nephew's behaviour, but the pregnancy must be kept a secret and the boy sent away at once. He must never set foot on that street again.

Ewah was relieved that he did not get the sack. The Chief had been a most generous employer. He was responsible for Ewah's children's school fees and had paid a deposit on a low-cost house for him. He was very upset that he had to send his nephew away, but what else could he do? If the boy had not been a pilferer, he would have arranged with a friend of his to take him in, but, as things were, he was unwilling to do that for it would have exposed the skeleton in the family cupboard. He gave Diba some money and told him to look for boys of his own age with whom he could share a room, and if he was in any difficulty he should contact a friend of Ewah's who would pass the message on.

Diba left but made up his mind not to contact any member of his family so as not to cause further embarrassment to anyone. He would have to find a job, look for accommodation and further his own education if he could.

He had been in Lagos for just over seven months and he had not made any real friends so, as he wanted to economise with what little money he had, he decided to **sleep rough** until things improved. As he roamed about Lagos, he thought of Toki. He liked her. She was not pretty but was quiet and fun to be with, and he had been flattered that she had sought his friendship even though she had been aloof at first. He was not sorry for her. Her parents had not rejected her whereas he had no one to turn to. He was not bitter, but he had been rather disappointed at the way the matter had been handled. No one, not even his uncle, had asked him for his own side of the story. It was as if he did not matter at all. Toki was listened to, a decision was made and he was asked to leave. He slept rough in motor parks, railway stations and in empty open sheds. He kept moving so as not to attract the attention of the police or night guards. What with mixing with **drug addicts, semi-lunatics and petty thieves**, in a few weeks he had toughened up considerably, both mentally and physically. He saw so many destitutes during that period that it was almost a surprise when he came across people who had homes to go to. Some of these apparent destitutes were actually perfectly respectable. Early in the morning you could find them near the lagoon cleaning up in preparation for going to their places of work. It was an eye-opener for Diba and he wondered why people stayed on in big cities in spite of the hardships. Could they be like him, rejected by their families for one reason or the other, or were they too ashamed to go back home and admit that they had failed to make it?

One day it dawned on him that he had **not pilfered** since he left his uncle's. Could it be that he had been too miserable to indulge in the habit, or had he not found anything that caught his fancy? Was it for fear of the police? He could not say. Just as his money was about to run out, he began to **sell newspapers** to support himself, and soon he was sharing a room in central Lagos with nine other vendors. Actually the room was only a place to keep their things in, and sometimes take a rest during the day as they usually slept around the newspaper distribution centres. It was a terrible life but he decided to hold on a bit until he had saved enough money to rent a room and look for something more decent to do. Soon, unfortunately, the old habit returned and his mates found their lost items in his possession. He was thoroughly beaten up, his things were seized from him and he was pushed out with only the clothes he had on.

That evening, while hanging about at the **Alayabiagba bus stop**, he stole out of necessity for the first time. He was hungry and had not a kobo on him, so he took a purse out of a lady's shoulder bag. Unfortunately, the lady noticed, raised the alarm and people gave him a chase. He was very frightened and as he cut across a field he threw the incriminating purse away and burst out onto a major road. Shouts of "**Ole, ole, thief, thief**," filled the air as his pursuers closed in. Someone tackled him and he fell down. A crowd gathered. More people poured in from other directions exclaiming, "Thief, thief!" "One of them has been caught." "Hold him fast." A middle-aged woman was pushed forward.

"Is this one of them?" someone asked her.

"Yes, yes," said the sobbing woman, hardly looking at Diba. "He was the one who stopped the car. His mates came out of hiding and attacked the driver, and they later drove off in the car."

Diba, who spoke no Yoruba, did not understand what the woman was saying and anyway, no one would have listened to him if he had attempted to defend himself. Unknown to him an **armed robbery** had just taken place in a side lane and a taxi driver had been stabbed to death. The crowd was incensed. Cases of armed robbery were very common in the area. He was beaten up until he was almost unconscious. His pursuers tried in vain to convince the crowd that all he had done was snatch a lady's purse and that he could not possibly have been involved in the armed robbery.

"A thief is a thief," said a man nearby. "If he could snatch a purse he could snatch a car."

"Let's **burn him** to teach others a lesson. This area is plagued with armed robberies. We never have a full night's rest. Robbers don't show innocent people any mercy."

"Yes, let's burn him."

"Bring an old tyre and some petrol."

"Here's a box of matches."

"Put the tyre around his neck."

It was the timely intervention of a patrolling team of **mobile policemen** that prevented his being burnt alive. The crowd was dispersed and he was revived and taken to a hospital where a police guard was put near his bed. It was a harrowing experience for him, but later he was glad that he had had the presence of mind to give the police his name as **'Andy Brown'** of no fixed address.

This did not help his case in the court as the judge distrusted people without a fixed address. He disbelieved everything Diba said in court and was very stern in his judgement. It was a sign of the times, he said, that a young man of Diba's personality and obvious good educational background should become an armed robber and go about terrorising innocent citizens instead of contributing something to the progress of the country. He was going to make an example out of him and he sentenced him to **fifteen years' imprisonment** on the evidence of the female passenger in the taxi cab.

Diba led a model life in **Damay Prison** in Lagos for about six years until the day there was a riot and he became excited and joined a group of prisoners who wanted to break out. They were recaptured and he was among those who were punished and transferred to prisons in other towns.

It was at the **Sabo Prison in Onitsha** that he met Flint. They were cell-mates and at first hardly spoke to each other. He was in awe of the older man who looked every inch the hardened criminal he was. He missed Damay Prison where the inmates had been mostly his age-group and communication had been easier. There had been vocational courses there and he had been pursuing a course in **catering and hotel management** when the riot had taken place. Here in Onitsha everywhere was drab and the inmates were hostile and eccentric.

After they had been together for two weeks, Flint discovered his cigarette lighter in Diba's possession and he dealt him a few sharp blows which sent the younger man cowering into a corner.

Later Flint felt sorry for the huddled figure. Usually he had no time for emotional display and he despised men who cried.

"Come, sonny," he said roughly but kindly. "Why did you do it? You don't smoke so what did you want a lighter for?"

Diba continued to sob.

"Was it to play with? A sort of toy?" he mocked. He knew that long stretches in prison sometimes brought on many psychological problems even in the most seasoned criminal. "Oh, for heaven's sake stop whimpering!" he admonished, beginning to lose his patience. "Are you a man or a mouse? How old are you and what are you in here for?"

"For armed robbery. I'm twenty-five."

"Well, well! Where's your manly

courage? I only dealt you a few light blows. You're supposed to be tough in your profession."

"But I'm not an armed robber," protested Diba feebly.

"Oh no? Neither am I," laughed the other sarcastically.

"I'm not," protested Diba vehemently, and thereupon he began to narrate how he had got put in prison. It was the first time he had discussed it with anyone. Flint listened attentively, grunting here and there. He was not surprised at all for it was not an unusual story. People got convicted sometimes for offences they knew nothing about.

"How sad," Flint said at last. "However..."

"Perhaps you don't believe me."

"Oh yes, I do. I could tell straight away that you were telling the truth. Since you joined me in this cell, I've always had the feeling that you were out of place. You just don't fit in with the usual crowd. Still, you were lucky that that crowd was prevented from burning you alive. I've witnessed with my own eyes two instances of innocent people being lynched by an angry mob for armed robberies in which I had taken part. I just mingled with the crowd and watched. It was pathetic but then life is always unfair. My policy is that you **grab what you can**."

"But isn't that all wrong? To kill and steal? I believe I'm being punished for all the pilfering I've done." "Ha, ha!" laughed the other. "Don't you believe a word of all that religious crap about punishment and hell. A good number of us robbers get religious leaders to pray for us so that our operations will be successful. We pay well for the service too. Those who don't believe in prayers go to **juju priests** for charms that will protect them from being caught or killed."

"Yes, but later we shall be called upon to account for our lives here on earth."

"By whom? Look, sonny, there's nothing like that. All that nonsense is an age-old trick to get the poor and the down-trodden to behave themselves well while the people at the top—whether in the government, business firms or religious bodies—cheat and enrich themselves. With a dash of the pen they commit robberies worth millions of naira and nobody condemns them. And if they are ever given a jail sentence they are treated as privileged prisoners and put in special cells. When they are released, they are welcomed straight back into society and life for them goes on very much as before. It's a pity you're straight. I could have taught you quite a few tricks of the profession. With your innocent good looks we could carry out some really big swindles."

"Oh no! I couldn't go on with that sort of life. My ambition has always been to train as a **lawyer**. That's gone down the drain now, of course. I can only dream about it."

"You're still young enough to realise that ambition. That is, if your luck holds and you keep out of trouble." "It's these itching fingers of mine. How can I ever study in a higher institution with this sort of defect? I would be found out and expelled. I might even land in jail again—perhaps that's the only sort of life I can ever look forward to. I wish I could control these fingers." He looked down at them miserably.

"It's a defect that's not easy to correct unless you're willing to make a big effort."

"I've tried."

"Try harder. We **professionals** look down on petty thieves. They are such a nuisance."

"I understand. Perhaps there are some of them who, like me, do not want to steal, but simply cannot help picking other people's things up."

"Maybe." An idea occurred to **Flint**. He yawned, got up and dropped his cigarette lighter. **Diba** bent down to pick it up for him, but in a swift movement Flint grabbed his wrist and gave it a twist and a wrench. Diba muffled a scream and fell back on his bed, writhing in pain.

"Never, never, pick up things which are not yours," growled Flint, waving a fist at him.

"I was going to pick it up for you," moaned Diba, when he could speak. He looked fearfully at his wrist which was swelling rapidly.

"I knew you were," laughed Flint. "This is the beginning of the lessons I intend to give you to help you stop pilfering. It worked with my cousin, and it might work with you too. I like you, and since your idea of a normal life is a clean, straight one, I'll help you in whatever way I can. Who knows? I might require your services in the future if you do qualify as a lawyer." Flint winked. Diba smiled doubtfully.

"Don't worry about your wrist, I'll beg a friendly warder to bring us some ice for it. Each time you feel the urge to pick up things, remember that excruciating pain in your wrist."

It was thus that a **solid friendship** sprang up between the two men, although they each viewed life from a different angle. Flint believed in luxury and dissipation. He led a reckless life, frittering away all his money on women, fast cars and high living. He told Diba he had made no provision for his future and did not want to get married.

"This is a horrible world to bring children into," he explained to his cell-mate. "It's hard and cruel and full of disasters. Besides, I wouldn't want my offspring to suffer in any way as a result of the crimes I've committed. If I died today, I'd have no regrets, for I've thoroughly enjoyed my life, but I'm damned if I'm going to leave money for others to enjoy."

"What about when you're old or incapacitated and can no longer lead this type of life? What will you do for money then?"

"Oh, there's always a way. I'll become a **receiver** and dispose of stolen goods and get my share of the booty." Flint laughed recklessly.

Diba learnt a lot from the older man,

who taught him how to cope with life, and protected him from the bizarre advances from other prisoners. He taught him to put up a bold front and meet his opponent head-on, even if he felt like jelly inside. That was how to survive. "Never let your opponent know that you're afraid. To give you courage, always think up something to despise in him. That fast-talking and tough-looking guy may be afraid of heights, spiders, the dark or lots of other things. He's flesh and blood just like you are."

Flint also encouraged him to take up **vocational courses**, so Diba continued with his catering course and sat for the **City and Guilds** examinations.

"If I fail to make it as a lawyer, then I'll run an eating place," he told Flint happily as he showed him his certificate.

"That'll suit me. I'll join you when I'm out, and have an office at the back of your restaurant from where I'll direct my operations. It'd be the perfect cover."

Diba laughed, hoping it was a joke.

Although he liked Flint immensely and was grateful to him for all his help, he intended to put a great distance between himself and the **criminal fraternity** once he was out of jail.

Already he had **stopped pilfering**. It was like a miracle to him. He did not know when exactly. One day Flint just drew his attention to the fact that he had not picked up anything for more than fourteen months. It has not been easy. Apart from the imaginary aching wrist each time he felt the urge, Flint made him return every article with an apology to the owner even when the theft had gone unnoticed. The situation embarrassed Diba so much that he became extremely self-conscious whenever he was alone outside his cell and thus refrained from touching anything. Soon the idea did not even occur to him. If he needed anything, he asked.

This made Diba more confident of himself and he began to make plans for when he was released from jail. As the time drew near, however, he became frightened.

What did the future really hold for him? Where could he go? Would people accept him freely in society? What about his family? Had they given him up for dead? Of course, no one knew what had happened to him or where he was, for he had been using an alias in jail.

"You're fretting over nothing," Flint told him. "I thought I had made a bold man out of you, but now, I'm not so sure. I can see you're going to have problems."

"Don't blame me, Flint. Of course I'll have problems. How will I fit into society? I was sent to jail ten years ago when I was in my teens. I've known no other adult life apart from that of prisons. I have no one to go to when I leave here. Absolutely no one."

"You could go to some friends of mine here in **Onitsha** and they'd look after you."

"I don't think I'd like to settle here in Onitsha." "What about **Port Harcourt**?"

"I'd like that, but not immediately. It's too close to my home town. I'd like to settle there or in **Calabar** when I'm earning a decent living and can take the risk of running into my relatives."

"Where will you go, then?"

"I don't know. I could go to **Lagos**, but I have no money for transport. There I could work as a cook or join a bakery or do any odd jobs for a start."

"All right, I'll give you a **hundred naira** and you can buy some clothes and other personal items. Since you don't want to go to my friends here in Onitsha, make sure you get a job which will give you accommodation. When you have more money you can find your way to Lagos and the bright lights."

"Will you really give me a hundred naira to start me off, Flint? That's the most generous of you." Diba was close to tears. "May the good Lord reward you a hundredfold."

He did not ask his friend how he came to have money on him in prison, for he had learnt not to ask such questions. Of all the inmates in their wing, Flint was the most affluent. He had everything he wanted and, in their four years together, Diba had never discovered his sources of supply. He simply accepted the money Flint peeled off a thick wad of notes he kept in a pocket sewn on the inside of his underwear.

"Alternatively," said his friend, and here he hesitated for a while, then went reluctantly on, "since you're bent on going back to Lagos, you could go to a relative of mine. She lives in **Aguda**. I'm doing this because I've come to look upon you as a son, and I'd like to help you all I can. This lady, **Mrs. Caro Oliga**, is a close relation who lives with her three children. She will help you. I am very reluctant to do this and I hope I'll never regret my action, but I think I'll risk it. I'll give you a note for her. I have never sent anyone to her for help before, but I'd hate to think of you destitute in Lagos."

There were tears of gratitude in Diba's eyes now at the other man's unselfish concern. If only he had been given such support by members of his own family, life would have been so much easier, he thought.

However, he decided not to take up an offer so half-heartedly given, and there was also his own decision to have nothing to do with criminals once he was released. He did not think that anyone associated with Flint could possibly lead a clean life. This relation of his was probably a receiver of stolen goods. Images of being stoned or burned to death by an angry mob came into his mind and he shuddered.

Both men tried to control their emotions the next day when a warder called to take Diba to the superintendent's office. They merely shook hands as the 'goodbyes' stuck in their throats. The superintendent spoke kindly to him and gave him a bundle containing the things that he had had when he had come to **Sabo Prison**. He was also given the addresses of two organisations he could contact for help with his resettlement. He made up his mind not to go to these voluntary organisations, for he had been told by other inmates that relations were usually contacted, first, before help was given. Funds were limited, so only those rejected by their families or who had no one were helped. The last thing Diba wanted was for anyone connected with him to know where he had been.

As the prison gates **clanged shut** behind him, he took a few steps and stopped to look at the high walls which had housed him for the past four or five years. He thought of the inmates and what they were possibly doing at that moment. He knew. They were waiting, waiting for something to happen, for most of them, like Flint, were in for life. They were forever plotting and planning their escapes. Occasionally one or two were successful in getting away, but many knew that they were likely to die in jail. Still, they kept hoping. Tough ones like Flint kept their spirits up by terrorising others in secret and doing all sorts of illegal things, but a few were pitiful to watch, especially those in solitary cells. Diba always trembled when he came across these men who had become **sub-human**. As he stood there, he wondered how he looked to people outside. Did his appearance give him away as someone recently released from prison? He was wearing the ill-fitting, used clothes that the authorities had given him. Usually relatives of prisoners were allowed to bring in fresh clothes for their release but, since he had nobody else to help, he had been given some. Without looking at the mirror he knew that he looked weird and unkempt and years older than his twenty-eight years. Despite Flint's pep talk, he still felt frightened at being free—free to go wherever he liked and do precisely what he wanted. He had become used to speaking only when spoken to, and accustomed to taking orders. He ought to be glad about his new-found freedom. He shook his head as if to clear it of cobwebs, and walked forward resolutely.

"Remember that people will react to you the way you present yourself to them, so always be on the alert and appear tough. Particularly here in Onitsha where everyone is extremely smart," Flint had told him as he left.

CHAPTER 2

He walked to the main road without a backward glance. It was a very busy road with lots of shops on both sides. There was a great deal of buying and selling being done on the pavements as well, and people jostled one another continually. Someone slipped a hand into his pocket. Diba caught the hand and gave it a twist and then released it. The owner quickly mingled with the crowd and disappeared. "**I must watch it**," he told himself. "**I'm really on my own now**."

He caught sight of himself in the glass of a shop window, and was shocked at what he saw. "Do I really look like that? An old young man!" His skin was pale and his hair was dirty grey. This, added to his ill-fitting clothes, made people give him curious glances. He had been wondering why one or two young ladies had deliberately moved out of his way on the pavement. "**I must do something at once! Have a haircut and a**

change of clothes! How far will the hundred naira go?" He had not used money for a long time.

He went into a barber's shop. The man took a look at him and his bundle and nodded towards a chair. Diba tried not to look at his own reflection until he had had the haircut and a shave, but this was difficult as he was surrounded by mirrors. As he wrapped a dirty sheet of white cloth around Diba's shoulders, the barber asked him how he would like his hair cut. He had deliberately chosen that particular cloth. The clean ones were reserved for customers who looked decent. This one certainly did not! Diba liked neither the state nor the smell of the sheet but was not going to make a fuss at first. Suddenly he rebelled against the whole situation. **Ex-convict or no ex-convict, I must assert myself and demand good service for the money I'm going to pay,** he thought.

"What style do you want?" asked the barber again. "A good one that will suit the shape of my head; something not too low.

Are you going to use this?" he asked, touching the dirty cloth.

"Yes, what's wrong with it?"

"It's dirty," said Diba feebly. Perhaps he should not make any fuss.

"So what? It's cleaner and newer than what you have on." Courtesy was not the man's strong point and this customer's appearance did not demand any.

"What did you say?" asked Diba, getting up from the chair. He was breathing hard. It was the first time in years that he had made a protest about anything. Had the barber guessed that he had just been released from jail? Sabo was only round the corner. All the same he knew that he must not miss his very first opportunity to be tough; he must set the pattern for his future behaviour. So he wrenched the sheet from his neck, threw it on the floor, spat on it and waited for the barber's reaction. The man was speechless and undecided.

"If you think," said Diba, shaking a fist at him, "that I'm going to pay **five naira**" (he had seen the price-list on the wall) "for a haircut and have that dirty sheet around my shoulders, then you must be mad. Raving mad! I shall disgrace you by taking that sheet out onto the busy street and telling all the passers-by what sort of service you give here. That should make your day and bring in more customers since you're the only barber in the whole of Onitsha."

The barber looked subdued. He knew that Diba was mocking him. His street and the surrounding ones had a large sprinkling of barbers and business was not at all good with all the sophisticated hairdressing saloons which were springing up all over the place. This man could ruin him if he carried out his threat. Moreover it was usually his policy never to miss a customer as he could be the only one for the day. He had many mouths to feed, but he had not been able to overcome the urge to play the snob that morning when Diba had walked in, looking every inch a society reject. He often did this when he had customers who had obviously come straight out of prison. It made him feel like a lord since they usually accepted such treatment the first time. This one was different. He became more conciliatory in his attitude.

"Sorry, **Oga**," he said, smiling nervously. He picked up the dirty linen and flung it into a corner, calling out to his daughter who was playing outside to take it home to her mother for washing.

"Sit down, Oga, don't be angry. Here's a clean sheet." He dusted the chair with a towel. Diba sat down. He was feeling weak and faint, but he mumbled some curses, glared at the barber and sprawled down in the chair. The slight confrontation had taken all his courage, but the victory was sweet. He shut his eyes and tried to think as locks of hair fell about him. Exhausted, he dozed off.

"Oga, do you want a dye and shampoo?" asked the barber, shaking him gently by the shoulder.

"Eh, what?" Diba rubbed his eyes. He got up and began to look at him. "Where's

my broom and pail? I keep them... Oh..." He
felt confused. Sleep cleared and he
remembered that he was no longer in
prison. "I'm sorry, eh, eh, you see," he tried
to explain to the other man as he sat down
again. **"I've just been released from jail
after a long stretch."** He was surprised at
himself for saying such a thing out loud.

The barber only smiled and nodded. "I
know."

"Is it that obvious?"

"It is." There was silence.

"Oga, do you want me to give you a dye
and a shampoo? It would make you look
better, and the ladies would not be able to
resist you. I can see now that you're a
handsome young man. It'll cost you an extra
five naira."

"All right, but I can only pay **N3**. I've no
money." "Okay, Oga, I want to help you. I'll
take N3. Maybe you'll patronise us again?"
After a short silence, during which he
attended to Diba's hair, the barber asked
him if he would not like a change of clothes.

"My wife sells **second-hand clothes**. Very nice and cheap. Almost new. Imported."

Diba looked at himself in the mirror. The man had done a good job. Oh, how he hated those ill-fitting clothes, but he was damned if he was going to kit himself out in second-hand clothes whose previous wearers he knew nothing about. Even as a child he had never worn them. It was different with prison clothes. He had had no choice. He would have to have something new but cheap. He rejected the man's offer and asked where cheap new clothes could be bought. The man brightened up at once and told him that his sister had a stall at the **Onitsha market** where she and her husband sold cheap family wear. All imported, he insisted. He gave Diba the address.

Adjusting to life outside prison was more difficult than Diba had anticipated. Crossing a busy road, for example, proved an **ordeal** and he was almost run down by vehicles several times. The experience left him all weak and trembling on the other side of the road. Flint had hinted that this might happen and that the best way to overcome this fear was to spend as much time in the streets as possible, crossing busy roads here and there. This helped.

Getting a casual job posed no problem at all, he was surprised to discover. He got one the day after he was released. He walked into one of the numerous bakeries in town and was offered a job on the spot. His employer did not even ask for references, and he was readily given accommodation on the premises when he said that he had just arrived from Port Harcourt and had nowhere to stay. Resident workers were usually welcomed by proprietors as they were available to be called upon to help out when there was a shortage of hands. This proprietor was particularly pleased with his 'catch' for Diba came in cheap at **eighty naira a month**. He must be new to the business or perhaps he was desperate for a job?

The work was boring and the hours long and tiring. Diba had done hard work in prison but it had been at a slow pace and there had not been so much talking to do. Here, the workers chattered endlessly, and when he failed to join in their discussions he was asked if he had a **speech impediment**. So, in order to become more acceptable in their circle, he tried to contribute to these conversations even though he had to put up with terrible attacks of **migraine** afterwards. He had to persevere because he knew that he was gradually becoming **integrated into society** and this made him happy.

Opposite the bakery there was a big hotel and, when work was slack, Diba enjoyed going over to chat with the gatemen, and watch the goings-on: cars of all makes and sizes zooming in and out of the gates to pick up or drop affluent-looking customers; pretty local and foreign girls hanging about for clients; neat waiters serving drinks and food on the well-kept lawn. It reminded him of his pre-jail life when as a visitor to Lagos he had made sure he visited all the most popular hotels.

The busy, sophisticated atmosphere

excited him and he began to dream of the time when he might have the opportunity of working in such a place, using his proper qualifications. With time and hard work he should rise to the position of manager and then be able to work his way up to the big hotels in **Kano, Lagos, Port Harcourt** and **Calabar**. For the moment, he decided he would save some money so that he could rent a decent room and apply for a job at the hotel. The owner, **Mr. Ifeanyi**, was a pleasant-looking man of about Diba's age. He was always well-dressed and it was rumoured that he was shortly to take a chieftaincy title in his village. Diba envied him. "What a lucky fellow to have so much wealth so young," he sighed wistfully.

A few weeks later, however, he had no more reason to envy him as the man was **mobbed and killed**, and his cars and hotel burnt down by the inhabitants of Onitsha in an uprising against armed robbers. It had all happened rapidly. One day the whole town seemed under siege, and the next the people had had enough. They had taken the law into their own hands and had gone about killing notorious armed robbers and their godfathers, and burning their property. No looting had been allowed to take place. Ill-gotten gains had to be destroyed. The police quickly brought the situation under control, but the people had had their revenge and were satisfied. It would be a long time before robbers would dare invade Onitsha again. They would have to carry their nefarious activities further afield, for even the people remotely related to them were publicly humiliated and some had had to go into hiding.

The incident left Diba almost a **nervous wreck**. It reminded him what had almost happened to him. He stayed in his room all day, trembling violently. His mates were amused and they plied him with hot drinks to pep him up. It did not help. He decided to move on as soon as possible. Five months later, he left for Lagos and went straight to the domestic quarters of Chief Laja's house to look for his uncle Ewah. He need not have disguised himself, for he was told on enquiry that all the Laja children had left home and the old couple were holidaying abroad. His uncle had retired to Calabar a year before. All the domestic helpers were aliens from neighbouring countries.

He stayed in a guest house on the outskirts of Lagos and tried to look for a job in one of the big hotels. This was frustrating as prospective employers who were impressed by his performance in the City and Guilds examinations could not employ him in a responsible post because he had **no experience and no references**.

Besides, there was no co-ordination in the names on his certificates: the **West African School Certificate** one had his real name on it, while the one issued by the City and Guilds had **'Andy Brown'** on it. He was in a fix unless he admitted to being an ex-convict and using an alias while in jail. He could not imagine anyone employing him with such a background. It made him ponder. **How were ex-prisoners supposed to get re-absorbed into society?** Perhaps he should contact the organisations recommended by the superintendent in Sabo Prison? Yet how would they be able to help him without getting him tagged as an ex-convict? Oh, how he loathed that word! How did people who had been to jail in other countries get back to leading a normal life? Was it possible? Political or privileged prisoners had no problems afterwards, he had been told.

Diba wished he knew someone highly placed in the government. He would have persuaded that person to make the **rehabilitation of prisoners** top of his list of priorities.

As he did not want to remain unemployed, Diba had to accept a position in a medium-sized hotel in **Ajegunle**. Unfortunately, it was a popular drinking place for criminals and it was constantly being raided by the police. He had to leave after the first month. It was the same in the three other places he worked in, and he gradually became more and more frustrated. He missed Flint and felt miserable and alone. He had been out of prison for over a year and things were going from bad to worse. He stayed in his room and did not look for another job. He fell ill and, when his condition became worse, his landlord asked what relatives could be contacted in Lagos or in any part of the country. When he said he had no one, his landlord told him that he would have to leave as he did not want a corpse on his hands. What explanation would he give the police if Diba were to die in his house? It was not as if he had enough money to pay for admission into a private hospital for more intensive attention. Diba was at his wits' end. The man was right. He had to protect his own interests, and it did not matter if loss of life was involved. Well, there was only one thing to do, and that was to contact **Flint's cousin in Aguda**. Although he knew that Flint had been very reluctant to give him the address, and would prefer it if he did not go there, he also knew that his friend was fond enough of him to be distressed at the news of his death. Besides, since he did not want to contact his own family, he really had no choice except, of course, to die in the streets. No provision was made in society for people in his predicament. At least none that he knew of.

CHAPTER 3

It was bright and lovely and the birds were singing in the morning. Diba left for **Mrs. Oliga's**, but there was no joy in his heart. Apart from being very ill and weak, he was worried about what sort of reception he would get from the lady and her children. Would she allow him to stay for a while on the strength of Flint's note, which was now over a year old?

The taxi-driver helped him out of the car, collected his fare and made a quick U-turn. Diba collapsed as he struggled with his suitcase through the gate which led to the house. A maid ran out to find out what was wrong. He tried to get up but collapsed again. Giving her the note he tried to speak but no words came out of his mouth. The maid raised the alarm and two men from the neighbouring houses came to help him indoors. During the next few days Diba was **oblivious** of where he was or what was happening around him as he drifted in and out of consciousness.

After reading Flint's note, **Mrs. Oliga** waited on Diba day and night with the help of the maid and her daughter **Ebi**, a twenty-three-year-old who worked as a **nurse** in a nearby private hospital. Mrs. Oliga's sons were still at schools in the northern part of the country.

Mrs. Oliga was a tall, slim woman of average looks and was in her early forties. She was always fashionably and expensively dressed in Nigerian attire, but there was a **sad look in her eyes** which wealth had apparently not been able to eliminate. She had been a widow for many years and was a major distributor to several breweries.

The note from Flint had been quite a surprise to her for, he had never sent anyone to her for help before. He had always been very protective towards her. She decided that Diba must be a special friend to him. Her heart thumped painfully as she thought of Flint. He was someone who held a special place in her heart, even though his haphazard visits usually unnerved her. She never knew what Flint was going to do next.

She would do her best to help his friend, she determined. It was nice to have somebody in the house who needed her. She had brought up her children to learn to look after themselves, but she had sometimes regretted this later as they had become so fiercely independent that she felt they did not need her any more. Ebi, for instance, right from the day she got her first salary had insisted on paying for her own keep, and had threatened to live on her own if her mother refused to accept the money. When they were home, the boys did not allow anyone else to tidy up their room and they did their own washing. It was all very nice but she felt less important in their lives.

They had not always been as affluent as this. There had been many anxious moments while Mrs. Oliga had struggled alone to bring up her children. She had been the only child of her own mother and, although she had half-brothers and sisters, she had been

the apple of her father's eye, for her parents
had been childhood sweethearts and her
father had only taken another wife because
her own mother could not have anymore
children. For years she had been the only
child in the house, petted and pampered by
all. She had no head for bookwork and had
heaved a sigh of relief when she left the
primary school. Her parents had not
insisted too much on her studying further.
She had, however, gone to learn
dressmaking at a popular female
dressmaker's in the suburb of **Port
Harcourt** where they lived. When she had
qualified at sixteen, her parents had bought
her a sewing machine but she had not been
eager to start her own sewing institute. She
was blissfully in love with a 'rake' as her
parents had put it. He was a handsome,
respectful young businessman. Her parents
had taken a dislike to him mainly because
they **distrusted businessmen**, and he was a
stranger in that part of the country. A
businessman's wealth was 'here today and
gone tomorrow,' they had pointed out to
their daughter and, since they did not want
their child to have to struggle to make ends

meet, they opposed the marriage. However, the couple had run away to **Enugu** where they had married and had their three children.

Mrs. Oliga's world collapsed the day she lost her husband. She was only twenty-four and had just had a baby. **Ebi**, their eldest child, was only five years old. She went back to live with her parents in Port Harcourt for a while and later left for **Lagos** where she earned a living as a dressmaker. It was not easy as Lagos was at the time full of sophisticated **'London trained'** dressmakers and the trend was towards western clothes. She specialised in **native attire** and it was when dresses began to acquire a 'Nigerian look' that her business picked up. This was what she had been hoping for, so she scrimped and saved and worked long hours.

When she had enough money for a deposit she decided to go into the **drinks business** - first on attachment, then as a dealer and finally as a distributor.

These days she could afford to sit back

and relax, for she had invested her money well in building houses for commercial purposes, and in other businesses. She knew that neither she nor any of her children would have monetary headaches for quite a while if they managed their finances well. She had been disappointed when all Ebi wanted to be was a **nurse**. She would have been very proud to have a daughter who was a lawyer or a doctor, but seeing how dedicated the girl was to her profession she had been pacified. The boys showed a lot of promise in their fields—one was studying **architecture** and the other **business administration**. Their father would be so proud of them, she thought.

Mrs. Oliga had had several male friends but had not remarried, for no man could ever have measured up to the husband who had showered her with so much love, care and what money he had. She did not really want a step-father for her children. Besides, she had started to get offers of marriage only after she had become successful in business. When she had first arrived in Lagos none of her male friends had shown any interest in taking on a ready-made family, and relationships had lasted for only a few months at a time. She had missed having a man in the house and was aware too that the children would benefit from having a father-figure. This was where her distant cousin, **Tamu**, a widower and a retired railwayman, had come in handy. He lived nearby and it was he who had disciplined the children when necessary, and escorted her to parties and tribal meetings. That way, things had worked out fine and she had been fairly happy, although she knew that some people in their social circle despised her for being without a husband despite her wealth. Some said she was an unmarried mother who had had her bastards in Enugu and had come to hide her head in Lagos. Tamu had told her that these people were **jealous of her success** and that she should learn to ignore their gossiping. She had done this, but there was still something missing in her life which total devotion to her children and her business had not been able to replace. That was **love**: the type she had shared with her husband. She needed to love and be loved by a man who was not after her money. Sometimes she would lie awake at night thinking about it and wondering if happiness of that kind was going to elude her for life. Fate had dealt her a cruel blow at too early an age and she hoped Ebi would be luckier whenever she chose to get married. For the moment, however, the girl was enjoying herself playing the field.

She sighed as she spooned some **pepper soup** into **Diba's** mouth. He had been there a week and was beginning to respond to treatment gradually, but was still too weak to handle cutlery properly. The doctor from Ebi's hospital had said that he was suffering from **undernourishment and depression**. The nourishment bit of it was easy, for all it entailed was seeing that he got enough good food and rest, but the depression bit of it defeated her. Diba clammed up whenever she asked him questions about himself and there was no way she seemed able to draw him out of his reticence. All she could get out of him was that he had met **Flint** at a party in **Onitsha** several years before and they had become firm friends. So when he had to come to Lagos, Flint had reluctantly given him her address and said that he could come to her for aid if he was desperate.

He had not contacted her earlier, he said, because he had not wanted to bother her, but when he lost his job and accommodation and became seriously ill, he had no choice but to come to her. She scolded him for his indifference. Even if he had not needed her help, he could have called on her all the same to say 'hello' for Flint's sake. He agreed with her and apologised. All efforts to get him to talk about his family and his past proved abortive, as he merely answered her questions with monosyllables or grunted. As he filled out and his feet became firmer on the ground, his appearance improved. She threw out most of his cheap clothes, which had become worn out anyway, and she told Tamu to buy him new ones. Flint had said in his note that he would refund whatever she spent on Diba. He had usually kept his word in the past, but even if he did not in this case, she would not mind, as what she was doing for Diba gave her a lot of satisfaction.

As he got much better, he began to talk about getting a job, and he, Mrs. Oliga and Tamu sat down to discuss his prospects. They were surprised when he rejected Mrs. Oliga's offer to contact various big organisations for a good position in their **catering or foods divisions**. Since he had the relevant qualifications she was sure she could help him get good employment. The experience bit would be waived, she assured him, and if he worked well, promotion would be rapid. He knew he was throwing away a good chance, but he also knew that these companies usually checked how genuine their employees' certificates were. What if it was discovered that **"Zone ZY,"** which had been the centre where he had sat for the examinations, was **Sabo Prison in Onitsha**? The company would carry out further investigations and it would come out that he had been jailed for **armed robbery**. The humiliation would kill him, and he would lose his new friends, who he had discovered were not only honest but were also totally unaware of Flint's real profession. They believed he was a **seaman**. If they too had been involved in criminal activities, things might have been easier to explain.

Ebi knew that she was strongly attracted by Diba's good looks and polite manners and that, given a little encouragement, she could easily become very fond of him. Those broad shoulders, strong arms and easy smiles were very inviting. She had liked him even when he had lain helpless on his sick bed, hovering between life and death, and she and her mother had had to perform some not very pleasant duties as they nursed him. But unlike her mother, who had seen him as an object on which to lavish care and attention to prove that she was needed, Ebi had seen him as a **man**, and had been conscious of every physical contact between them.

As he got better and gradually became an active member of the household, she liked him more, but was disappointed when she realised that all his attention was focused on pleasing her mother. He hovered around Mrs. Oliga and couldn't seem to do enough for her. At first Ebi thought he was only showing his gratitude for the care he was receiving, but then she began to suspect that he had some **ulterior motive**. After all, she too had nursed him, and yet he had made no special effort to strengthen their relationship. He must be after her mother's money, and what better way was there of laying his hands on it than worming his way into her affections and gaining her confidence? This disgusted her. Yet he looked a proud man and had an air of dignity about him; she could not really say that something improper was going on. All the same she found herself becoming suspicious of him, and when they were together she was snappy and irritable. This, of course, was exactly the opposite of what she wanted their relationship to be. She would have liked him to see what a warm, humorous and good-natured girl she was, just as other people did, but what came across was a hostile attitude. Try as she would, she could not behave any other way towards him to erase this impression. He did not complain but tried to keep out of her way as much as possible. This only made her more mad at him and at herself.

"I'm sure he has something to hide," she said to her mother and Tamu one day. "Have you noticed the way he grunts and averts his eyes whenever you talk to him?"

"He's probably shy among strangers. He's been here only seven weeks. Remember? And he's been ill in bed most of the time," said Mrs. Oliga.

"And we know next to nothing about him. He's probably a thief or an escaped lunatic. You watch it! We'll all be murdered in our beds one of these days, now that he can move about."

"I don't think things will be as bad as that," said Tamu pensively.

"Won't they, Uncle?" asked Ebi dubiously. "Well, starting from tonight I'll lock my door and put a table behind it. I advise you to do the same, Mum."

Her mother laughed. "Thank you, dear, but I don't think Diba is any of those things.

Maybe he's had some misfortune which alienated him from his family and affected his health. He needs a lot of help from us all. If Flint says he's okay, he is. He's not actually done anything to make us suspicious of him. He's very religious. He sleeps with the **Holy Book under his pillow**, and he's tried several times to give me religious lectures."

It was Ebi's turn to laugh. "Ah! My old teacher told us that the devil was very good at quoting from the Bible. Mum, I think you're just being nice and sentimental as usual. You enjoy mothering people, but be careful this time. Frankly, I should chuck him out, if I were you."

"What would your Uncle Flint say?"

"He wouldn't know and anyway we hardly see him anymore these days. He's probably away at sea again."

"Is he still a seaman, Caro?" asked Tamu, turning to Mrs. Oliga. "I thought you said he had retired and had set up business somewhere near the **Cameroon border**."

"That was what he told me he was going to do the last time I saw him. However, he would be extremely displeased if I sent away the only person he's ever sent to me for help. He's said that he will be responsible for whatever money I spend on Diba." "Hm! Well, the Lord will protect us all from evil."

"Amen."

CHAPTER 4

Mrs. Oliga liked Diba immensely. Apart from the fact that he made her feel needed again, he made her come alive as a woman. He was fond of paying her compliments on her appearance. She did not mind whether it was flattery or not. It made her feel good and it brought back happy memories of her days with her husband.

"The way you talk, you would make a very successful dress designer," she teased him when he commented on her choice of material, colour and style.

"Thank you, Madam, but I'd rather be a **lawyer**," he told her.

"Call me '**Auntie**', Diba. 'Madam' makes me sound old and austere."

"All right, Ma, er, Auntie."

"That's better. Why do you want to be a

lawyer?" "It's always been a dream of mine, but, thinking about it now, it would be too long a time before I could qualify and I want to be able to support myself as soon as possible."

"You're welcome to stay here for as long as you want to."

"Thank you, Auntie, that's very generous of you, but the earlier I stand on my own feet, the better. Then I can make other plans."

"We'll get something for you. Let's see, why don't you work for me at one of the **distribution centres**? I've just remembered that the clerk (well, we call him manager) in charge of the **Lagos Island** branch is leaving in September for further studies at the **University of Ife**. You can take his place when he goes. Meanwhile you could understudy him."

"Can I?" asked Diba doubtfully. "I've never done anything in the drinks line and I don't want to be a disappointment to you. Catering and hotel management duties are what I know I can do with a lot of confidence."

"Oh, there's nothing difficult about managing a drinks centre. You could do it in your head. All it involves is seeing to it that our retailers get adequate supplies, making sure of regular deliveries from the breweries and generally supervising other workers there. There's some **book-keeping** involved too, but perhaps—?"

"I'm good at figures. That'd be no problem, that is, Auntie, if you'd really consider giving me the job." "I've already made the offer, Diba," said Mrs. Oliga gently.

"It's eagerly accepted, Madam," he replied, getting up excitedly and going towards her. To his surprise, she embraced him, kissed him on the cheek and laid a hand on his shoulder. "You'll enjoy working for me, Diba. I appreciate hard work and, above all, **honesty**. The position entails handling a lot of money and that's a temptation for any young man. But I trust you," she added and, smiling into his eyes, she left the room.

Her comment left him feeling weak and a little bit shaky. Why had she talked about honesty? Did she suspect he had been to jail? He had stopped pilfering, but would the habit return? He had never stolen money; he had only picked up things he fancied. Did she know that her cousin Flint was a notorious armed robber?

That night, as they were both watching the television, there was a news item about an armed robbery in **Agege**; the suspect had been **burnt to death** that afternoon by the residents. Some pictures were shown. The effect of the scene was too much for Diba who uttered a cry and began to **tremble violently**. Mrs. Oliga was alarmed. She rushed out, got him some water to drink and sat down on the couch with him, patting his hand and trying to calm him down. She could not understand what could have brought on his 'shakes'. It had happened twice while he was ill. She frowned thoughtfully. She still did not think he was a criminal, but she would have given anything to know what could have happened to him in the past to reduce him to such a state. She decided she would not mention the incident to Tamu or Ebi as it would only heighten their suspicions.

After about a quarter of an hour, when he had recovered, he thanked her and said he was going to bed. She got up too, still holding and patting his hand. Just then Ebi, who had been out seeing friends, walked in. She was not surprised at what she saw. She had long suspected that the two might be lovers. The thought infuriated her.

"Hello, Mum," she greeted, sitting down and kicking off her shoes. She glared at Diba and then ignored him. Disgusting! A **fortune-hunter**! She was very fond of her Uncle Flint but she would never forgive him for sending this intruder to them to disrupt their peace, for she could feel a storm gathering somewhere. When it would burst would be a matter of how soon Diba could stash away enough of their money before he disappeared. It would serve her mother right. At her age and with her experience she should know better. It was not as if the man was all that good-looking. There was an age gap too!

"Ah, there you are, Ebi," said her mother with obvious relief. She released Diba's hand. "Come and take Diba's temperature or pulse or whatever you nurses call it. He feels unwell."

Ebi cocked an eye at Diba. "He looks all right to me," she said with indifference, not budging from her chair. "How can you tell from that distance?" admonished her mother. "He almost fainted a few minutes ago."

From passion, seethed Ebi inwardly.

"I'm all right, Auntie," said Diba, making as if to leave the room. "The heat was too much for me. It made me feel weak."

"The air-conditioner is on and the room is very cool," pointed out Ebi, with some asperity.

"Stop being unkind, Ebi," scolded her

mother. "**Florence Nightingale** would be ashamed of you," she added, trying to make light of the situation and bring out the good humour in the girl. "A nurse is always ready to help others." She knew this would prick the girl's conscience, for she was a dedicated nurse.

Ebi got up and led Diba to his room. She took his pulse and told her mother there was no cause for alarm. All he needed was a good sleep. She left the room to make him some cocoa.

Diba slept soundly that night but he woke up to a throbbing headache. He took some aspirins and lay down again, thinking. He had a problem to which an immediate solution must be sought. Flint had told him he should always meet his problems head-on, analyse them and try to find solutions. "**Never let problems weigh you down. That will age you and give you hypertension**," he had said.

Now his problem was **Ebi**. In detective books, Ebi would be eliminated in one way or the other, and the hero would plod on to a happy-ever-after ending, but he couldn't do that. She was the daughter of the house and he was the intruder. He had felt her intense dislike for him right from the start. Those slightly bulging eyes of hers would bore into you as if trying to read your innermost thoughts. They made you feel guilty even if you'd done nothing wrong, he thought. She was a likeable girl who was usually warm to most people, but she stalked him as if wanting to catch him at 'something'—what, he could not fathom exactly. She made him extremely nervous and jumpy. Her brothers were more friendly. After the initial feeling of shock at finding a stranger installed in their home in their absence, they took to him, dragging him all over Lagos with them. They taught him how to drive before Mrs. Oliga paid for driving lessons for him. He could tolerate Tamu, who pretended to mind his own business but was fiercely protective towards Mrs. Oliga and kept a sharp lookout for anything that might hurt her.

Diba was very fond of Mrs. Oliga, who reminded him of **Rebeccah**, who had been a neighbour of theirs in **Ukum**—tall, elegant and with a husky voice. He enjoyed being with her and they chatted easily together. She regarded him as one of the family and made him feel welcome. He still could not bring himself to confide in her about his past as he felt it might lower whatever regard she had for him; it was important to him that she should admire him and think him clever. Now that he was going to work for her he would do his best so that he would eventually become her right-hand man, and install himself firmly in her good books. He wanted to stay on in her employment until he had saved up for that restaurant which he planned to establish in **Calabar** or **Port Harcourt**—that is, if Ebi's hostile attitude did not disrupt his plans and make him leave before he was ready. Trying to become friendly with her had not yielded any results as she rebuffed all his moves. It had hurt his pride and, if he had had some money, he would have moved out of the house there and then. Yet, looking back, he was glad he hadn't, for he would have lost the offer of a good job which he needed badly. All he would do, he told himself, was to **assert himself and play tough with the girl**. No more cringing or trying to please her. He was no more a criminal than she was! Come to that, she was the relative of a notorious armed robber even if she was unaware of it. She had no reason to despise him! He was no coward, whatever else he was. He hoped, though, that this attitude would not offend the mother who was going to be his benefactor. He would have to go carefully.

CHAPTER 5

The job was not as easy as Mrs. Oliga had described. Diba was on his feet most of the day either in the shop or going from brewery to brewery. Sometimes he travelled out of Lagos to chase up deliveries. He was happy. He was on a good salary and he enjoyed the work. He looked forward to coming home in the evening to a good meal, for Mrs. Oliga spared no effort in looking after him. She came home earlier now to be with him. She would not hear of him contributing to his keep and he had not insisted as he needed to save all he could. Within six months he was made **General Manager of Oliga & Sons**, and although his office was still on Lagos Island, he was now the overall supervisor of the six distribution centres in town. He had become her right-hand man and he felt he deserved to be.

Even **Tamu** had to admire the young man's able management and hoped that he would not be tempted to swindle the company; he still kept a watchful eye on Diba. He had vowed years ago that, while he had breath in him, no one would cheat Caro after she had suffered so much to build up her business. Over the years he had personally had to chase away several troublesome fortune-hunters who had hung around her. His devotion to her was entirely without self-interest. He only wanted her to be happy after an earlier life of disillusionment. He did not need her money. He was a man of simple needs who led a contented, retired life just watching the world go by.

"Caro," he said one day to his cousin. "Now that you have an apparently honest and dedicated General Manager, why don't you do less work and enjoy life more? You still go round the centres daily. That's totally unnecessary. You'll kill yourself."

"What else can I do? You know how I hate to be idle." "There must be other things you'd like to do that would not involve the business. Something you've always wished you had time for; a hobby, journeys and so on."

"Tamu, you're right, you know," she answered after a few moments' thought. "There are lots of things I would like to do. Things like crocheting, gardening, keeping poultry, shopping at leisure and going more often to Port Harcourt to see my parents. I could make a whole list of things."

"Do so and get on with it. Do these things now while you are healthy and young enough."

"Thank you, Tamu. I'll start this week with a visit to my parents. My mother will be delighted to see me. I'll ask Diba to book a seat for me on the first flight on Saturday. I hope he'll be able to cope while I'm away."

"He should be able to. What's he being paid all that money for? If you like I could do your rounds," Tamu offered half-heartedly. He hated anything that involved roasting in Lagos's 'go-slow' traffic.

"No, no, the boy might be offended. Let's show him that we trust him and have confidence in his ability."

"I agree with you," Tamu said, thoroughly relieved.

Diba almost fell flat on his face as he slipped on the brown envelope which had been pushed under his office door. It bore no name or address, only "**Read this, sonny**." Now, there was only one person who called him 'Sonny'. That was **Flint**. His heart skipped a beat. He had been out of prison for almost two years now and had been living with the Oliga's for ten months. He had heard nothing from Flint and Mrs. Oliga hardly ever mentioned him.

The note was very brief and was in Flint's laborious handwriting. *"Sonny! Long time! The plans I told you of fell through. Don't worry, however, you'll see me soon. Carry on the good work you're doing at my cousin's. We'll set up that restaurant shortly. See you!"*

Diba was sorry to hear that Flint had not succeeded in escaping from jail, for he knew how he loved unrestricted movement. It was also sad to realise that Flint's freedom at any time would mean disaster for society, for no sooner would he be out than he would resume his criminal activities. Diba was ashamed to note his relief at his friend's continued stay in prison. Flint had done so much for him, yet Diba really did not want any further association with him. But how could he possibly avoid that? He lived with and worked for Flint's relatives. He felt trapped as he thought of Flint's likely escape from jail. He might never succeed, yet if he did he would certainly contact Diba. How could he shield a criminal on the run? If Flint were to be lawfully released, that would be another matter.

Diba stayed locked away in his office all afternoon, lost in thought. By early evening, he had made a decision. He would quit Mrs. Oliga's residence as soon as possible. Actually he had made up his mind to do that when he had discovered that he had **fallen in love with Ebi**. It had happened gradually and he had done his best to suppress the feeling. It was a hopeless situation he found himself in, for he was aware that neither Flint, nor anyone else for that matter, would believe that he was genuinely in love with her. He would be termed an **opportunist and a fortune-hunter**. And he would not blame them for their attitude. How would Flint take it? He would surely feel betrayed. The man had been reluctant enough to send him to the Oliga's in the first place. He had probably anticipated this sort of thing. No, he would keep his feelings to himself and move out as soon as he could afford to. Besides, Ebi obviously did not care a hoot about him and probably thought him the scum of the earth because of his impecunious condition. It was not easy, however, as each time he saw Ebi, the urge to take her in his arms, and tell her how much he loved her, grew stronger and stronger. It was torture, too, when she went off on dates with other men. Only the thought of going to jail prevented him sometimes from picking a fight with some of these men out of sheer jealousy, and venting his frustration on them.

The sensible thing to do was to live elsewhere. He would also have to look for another job before Flint contacted him again. He hoped Mrs. Oliga would not be difficult about releasing him and giving him a good reference. You could never predict her actions. She could be all sweetness and light one minute and the next, she would give you a good telling-off without a backward glance. He knew that she enjoyed flattery, so he dished it out regularly and, when she flirted sometimes with him, he responded cautiously even though he was aware that it was all harmless and she did the same with Tamu and other close friends. Mrs. Oliga was very secretive about her relationship with men and Diba could not tell whether she had a lover or not. She enjoyed the mystery that surrounded the issue.

Had she received a letter from Flint too? Had he said anything about Diba in it? The thought worried him.

Later that evening when she had gone round to Tamu's, Diba went to her room to have a quick look. She sometimes left it unlocked. He was in luck—the door was half-open.

It was a large, well-furnished and very

feminine room. There was a strong smell of lavender in the air. He did not know where to start looking for a letter. Even though he had been in the room before on errands he was not familiar with where things were kept. He went to the dressing table which was crowded with the usual female bits and pieces. A jewellery box stood open; on the very top of its contents lay a **diamond-encrusted gold cross**. He picked it up, fascinated by the thousands of fiery lights that winked at him. As he was about to put it back a voice close to his shoulder said, "Lovely, isn't it? It cost Mother a little over **ten thousand naira**."

Diba dropped the cross back in the box and whirled round to face Ebi who was wearing a happy, satisfied look on her face.

"Oh, hello Ebi, I thought you were out," he said, trying hard to control his heartbeats. He felt like taking her into his arms and planting a passionate kiss on those full lips. When he saw the half sneer on her face, he decided to give her his **slow confident smile**, which she found so maddening. She preferred his old furtive glances, which had made her feel in command of the situation.

"I'm sure you did, otherwise you wouldn't be in here," she told him coldly.

"What do you mean? I've been in this room before."

"Oh yes?" she asked, arching one eyebrow. "What for, if I may ask?"

"Your mother told me to fetch her something. But do I have to explain everything to you?" He had to play tough.

"Yes."

"Why?"

"Because," she said slowly, emphasising each word, "this is my home and you have no business in my mother's room. Get it?"

"Oh, I see. Well, I was just leaving," he said, trying to get past her. She barred his way. She was very conscious of his nearness and somehow expected him to take her by the shoulders, shake her or do anything to break down the barrier of her pretended hostility. A more discerning man would have done just that, and she would have welcomed the opportunity to cling to him and let him know that she was not indifferent to his personality. Instead he just stood there with an undefined expression on his face. He tried to get past again.

"Not so fast, Mister. You are going to stay right where you are until my mother arrives."

"Don't be ridiculous," Diba laughed. She liked that. "Why the room arrest?"

"Because I caught you red-handed, **stealing from my mother's jewellery box**," she said ungraciously. She did not know what made her utter such a statement. Perhaps she hoped it would put him in her power?

"I beg your pardon!" he shouted, feeling extremely offended. The girl was really going too far! He felt like shaking her. Yet he must be cool. "Ebi, could you repeat what

you've just said? You caught me doing
what?"

"Stealing from..." She was not going to
start apologising for what she had said. A
quarrel with him was better than his
indifferent attitude towards her.

"Listen, Ebi," he said, cutting in. "If I
wanted to steal from your mother I could
have done so effortlessly in the course of
business. I handle thousands of naira for her
and I have never stolen a kobo from her.
Why should I go to the trouble of coming to
her bedroom to steal jewellery, of all
things?"

"It's easier to slip into the pocket and to
dispose of, that's why. Theft from the
business would be quickly detected since
you'd naturally have to account for the
money."

"You're being ridiculous, Ebi. Your
mother trusts me implicitly."

"Does she now? Wait until I tell her
what has taken place this evening. You'll be
thrown out in no time."

They stood staring at each other, whatever anger they had tried to express melting away. He did not actually believe that she suspected him of theft, yet why had she been stalking him? His thoughts wandered to how lovely she looked with that defiant look on her face. She stood stiffly, waiting for him to make a move.

Just then the front door banged and Mrs. Oliga came into the room. She seemed preoccupied and expressed no surprise at seeing both of them there.

"Oh, hello, you two. What an evening I've had! I feel absolutely whacked! **Tamu's ill** and as usual he is very difficult about taking his medicine."

"What's the matter with him, Mum?" asked Ebi. She liked Tamu. "He was all right when I called there on my way to work this morning."

"He's got a bad headache and he says he can see funny little men with red hats dancing everywhere in the house."

"It might be something serious. Perhaps

he has a fever and is confused."

"I don't think so. If you ask me, I think he's had too many of those gins of his."

"Oh, he's been drinking again, has he?"

"I'd better go to him," offered Diba.

"No, don't go. There's something I want to discuss with you. Ebi, be a darling and go to Tamu. He kept asking for you and his children. He thinks the end is near. Ha! Ha! You might be able to force some **pepper soup** down him. He absolutely refused to have any while I was there."

"Er, er," hesitated Ebi. She hated the way she was being dismissed, but if Tamu had refused to have pepper soup he could be seriously ill, for it was his favourite pick-me-up. Should she tell her mother what Diba had been up to?

"Er, there's something I would like you to know, Mum. I came in here and found..."

Her mother was only half listening. She was at her dressing table taking off her ear-rings.

"Did I leave my jewellery box open and the door of my room unlocked? It's a good thing the maid is away in **Port Novo**. My goodness! The poor girl would have been tempted to help herself. I'm becoming very careless these days."

"As a matter of fact," began Ebi. She was determined to expose the scoundrel. "I..."

Diba cut in quickly. "I found the door open as I was passing by, and the cross at the top of the jewellery box caught my eye. I could not resist picking it up and admiring it." He was damned if he was going to upset his plans for the future. He was back at the dressing table now, standing very close to her. He picked up the cross again, exclaiming at the beauty. "It's beautiful. Really exquisite."

"Is it?" Mrs. Oliga asked, pleased. "Here, try it on." She put it on a gold chain and then around his neck. She stood back to admire it. "It looks very nice on you," she said, patting him on the cheek.

Ebi left the room in annoyance as Diba returned the cross to the box.

"It's **fake** though," her mother was saying. "The real one is in the bank. I bought this one for only a hundred naira in a shop in **Balogun Street**."

"Disgusting! Really disgusting the way they are carrying on," Ebi said to her friend **Adesuwa**, while at work the next day.

"Who?"

"My mother and Diba."

"You're on again about them?"

"Yes." Ebi described the scene in her mother's bedroom.

"Hm, he's a very smart fellow, beating you to it like that," mused her friend. "Look, why not try to trust him? He's right, you know. If he wanted, he could swindle your mother and run away before being detected. Besides, they are both adults and must know what they are doing."

"I hope so. You see, Mother is absolutely

infatuated. They behave like teenagers. She asked me the other day if I thought she would look nice in a **trouser suit**! She's never worn one in her life!"

"What's wrong with that?"

"At her age?"

"She's not old at all. She's only in her early forties or so, but you're trying to make her sound like **Methuselah**."

"He must be in his late twenties or early thirties." "Still, does it really matter? It's their affair. If it makes your mother happy to have a younger man for a lover, that's her business. Your main concern should be that she's happy."

"He's only after her money."

"Let your mother be the judge of that. There may be nothing at all between them. Your mother has always been very discreet about her affairs."

"I'm just afraid that in a moment of passion she might will everything she owns to him. They might even get secretly married. It's been known to happen before and he seems pretty desperate to me."

Adesuwa looked alarmed now. She would not like something like that to happen in her own family. Hard-earned family money being coolly taken over by a stranger? It was unthinkable.

"Why don't you discuss this point with your brothers and Uncle Tamu? They would know what to do. On the other hand, you could leave things as they are. Your mother has a right to be happy. She's suffered enough. Even if they were married it might not be a bad thing. Personally, I like Diba. He's gorgeously handsome and not a bad sort."

"He may not be a bad sort but he certainly likes a comfortable life."

"Naturally! Still, leave them to it. Your mother has been dodging fortune-hunters for a long time and ought to be able to smell them a mile off. She loves her children very much and I doubt if she would do anything foolish. You've never been this worried about her before."

"That's true. I'm probably more sensible now. Look, let's talk about something more interesting. How was last night's date?"

"Simply wonderful. **Ikponmwonsa's** so nice. He takes nurses seriously and doesn't think, like many of our men do, that they are just play-mates for doctors."

"Hm, I can smell a marriage proposal somewhere."

"Me too, but I'm going to give him the run of his life to test his endurance. Ha! Ha! When we are married he won't be as soft and nice as he's being now. Men always change for the worse later. How's the Prince?"

"**Princewill's** fine," replied Ebi. "He's gone away to Port Harcourt for a week and I miss him so much."

"Ah! Now I understand why you have time for the little problem at home!"

When Diba told Mrs. Oliga that he was going to move into a flat of his own, she did not protest. She was going to miss having him around but she was sensible enough to realise that he needed more privacy.

Ebi was so delighted at the news that she stayed in some evenings to help her mother make curtains for Diba's flat and, finally, helped him move. Since their encounter in her mother's bedroom, she had come to the conclusion that he was not interested in her. To hide her chagrin she began to have lots of dates, and to pretend that she was having tremendous fun.

"Boy, what a relief!" she told Adesuwa, shortly after Diba moved. "**Rejoice with me ye heavens, the pest has finally gone**."

"Oh? I'm glad for you."

"Thanks, dear. There'll be no more big brother/step-father to query my late home-coming."

"Was he doing that?"

"Oh, yes. Can you believe it? He made it his business to wait up for me each night I was out and tell me how worried my mother was whenever I came home late. I told him not to interfere in my affairs. He's a lousy liar."

"Why?"

"Because my mother would never lose her sleep over the hours I keep. You're aware of that."

"Yes, of course. But perhaps she did worry occasionally."

"Mother would have called me to order if she had been worried. Anyway, I told him off properly on each occasion. You'd be surprised! But he would still be waiting up the next time. He said I was behaving irresponsibly and that I would give my mother hypertension. Me, irresponsible? Just imagine that!"

"Hm!" said Adesuwa thoughtfully. "I'm not trying to defend his actions, but if he and your mother are as close as you said, he's in a good position to know her state of mind. So he might be genuinely concerned about her health."

"That's a thought. I would hate to hurt my mother's feelings. Still, I disliked the step-father role he was assuming. He's only a few years older than I am. Now, Uncle Tamu's not like that."

"He's never lived in the house."

"He knows all that goes on, all the same." Not for the life of her would she admit to her friend that she had fallen in love with Diba. She did not realise it herself until he had left the house. She felt bereft now that he was no longer there. Even the relationship with Princewill, who was top of the list of her boyfriends and of whom she had always been very fond, lost its glamour.

Diba still called at the house from time to time, but it was usually in the company of other girls. It made her acutely jealous when these girls flirted openly with him. Her mother did not seem to mind; indeed she welcomed him and his companions and entertained them at her parties.

CHAPTER 6

Although the rent and other bills cut deep into his salary, Diba was quite sure he had made the right decision in moving out. He was not necessarily happier, for though he now saw less of Ebi he was still very much in love with her. However, he enjoyed more freedom and privacy and was able to widen his circle of friends and have guests home whenever he wished. He was settling down well and only the thought of **Flint's** probable escape from jail gave him some anxiety. He would have to start looking for another job. Would a change of jobs keep Flint away? Would he not regard Diba's action as treacherous?

There was a knock on his office door one afternoon and an attractive, casually dressed lady came in.

"Good evening," she greeted him. "I'm sorry to bother you, but everyone around here said only you could help me." Diba did not reply; he was so deep in thought that he stared fixedly before him.

The lady hesitated and repeated her sentence. Diba shook his head and apologised.

"Good evening, Madam. Please sit down. What can I do for you?"

"I know you don't retail drinks, but I'm in a fix. I'm giving a party tonight and the man who was going to supply the drinks and food said he did not get the order which I made personally a fortnight ago. He says it's too late to do anything now. What shall I do? You must help me please, or I'm sunk."

"Well, we can help out with the drinks. Do you have any empty bottles?"

"That's another problem. I don't have any, but I could leave a deposit for them."

"The bottles are more important to us."

"I give you my word that I'll return them tomorrow morning. I live only three streets away. Please help me," she pleaded.

"All right. What types of drinks do you want?" She made her order, thanking Diba profusely. "You've saved my life. I'll collect some now and come back for the others later."

"Don't worry. I'll ask one of my boys to deliver them and help you unpack."

"Thanks. That'll be a great help. Here's the money. Please, do you know where I can get **small chop** at short notice?"

"We run a catering service in **Surulere** but I don't know if they can still supply you tonight. However, let's try and find out from the supervisor. I'll ring her up."

The phone call was made and the order taken. As she was leaving, she turned and invited Diba to her party. "You must come," she told him when he hesitated. "You've been so very kind to me."

"All right, Madam, I'll come. I hope your husband won't mind an intruder."

"I'm not married."

"Oh, I'm sorry. I thought..."

"No, you're not sorry," she teased. "I can read it in your eyes. I'll be expecting you. The party starts at nine, that is, if you're free and your wife..."

"I'm not married."

"I'm sorry, I..."

"No, you're not," he laughed. "I'll be there later."

As he dressed for the party, Diba was thoughtful. He could feel a new chapter in his life unfolding; one which involved the past and which was likely to have much influence on the future. Just how much influence he could not tell yet. Tonight, he would mix with people from a different social circle to the one he had been used to. Who knew, contact with these people might be of use to him in business later. Whatever their educational background might be, he knew he would not feel inferior in their midst. He was a good listener and conversationalist. He looked at his reflection in the mirror and smiled as if at a secret thought. On the way, he stopped to buy a bottle of wine for the lady. She had told him that she was a lawyer and was celebrating a change of jobs in these hard economic times. When he saw the **tastefully furnished flat** and the expensive presents on the table, he shrank a bit and felt like turning back. "Hold up your head, old boy," he admonished himself, "or you're going to miss an opportunity of meeting some potentially useful people."

The room was half full of chatting guests. He looked hesitantly round for the lady. The moment she saw him she pounced on him.

"Ladies and gentlemen!" she announced, clapping her hands for silence and raising Diba's hand. "**This is the gentleman I spoke to you about. The knight in shining armour who rescues damsels in distress.** When my fate hung in the balance, and all hope was lost, he gallantly stepped in and saved the situation. I declare him the hero of the evening. Please give him a round of applause and a seat of honour."

There was much clapping and Diba

found himself lifted up and deposited in a white cane chair. Someone pushed a glass of iced beer into his hand. He took a grateful sip and began to chat with those around him. There was a man in his late fifties who seemed out of place in the young gathering. He was quite handsome but short and a little pot-bellied. He was dressed in a silk **buba and trousers**, and sat in a conspicuous corner drinking **gin and lime**. He smiled benevolently on the guests and would occasionally call the hostess over and whisper something in her ear. She seemed to enjoy this, in between flirting with some of the young men in the room. The party swung gaily on.

"Who's the old boy in the corner?" asked one female guest of her neighbour. "Is he part of the furniture?" The other laughed. "He's **Tokunboh's** old man."

"I see. Why did she have to invite him to this party? To dampen it? I can't relax and enjoy myself with him looking on. He reminds me of my old headmaster and my father, rolled into one."

"I feel like that too. It is as if the eye of authority is on us and we are kids once more. Tokunboh didn't have to invite him. He's always here. Even his wife knows where to find him when he's not slaving away in his office."

"Ah, it's like that, is it? How can Tokunboh stand it?"

"She has to. After all, he pays for this posh flat, he's responsible for her shopping at the world's capitals and he's just bought her a **Mercedes sports**."

"He's that rich, is he?"

"Yes. He owns a chain of companies and practically swims in money!"

"Really?" the other asked, looking at the man with more interest and trying to catch his eye.

"Don't give him the 'come-on' look. It would be wasted. He's head over heels in love with his family and Tokunboh."

"Is he now? Still a girl can try, even if it's only to help him spend some of his money. It might be a refreshing change from Tokunboh and his wife, who knows? I'll go and chat with him for a while."

"Good luck," laughed her friend.

"Come in, Tokunboh," said Diba when she called at his flat some weeks after the party. They had been in contact earlier and had agreed to meet at his place. He fixed a drink for her, put on a record and they danced in silence for a while.

Two pleasant hours later, when she told him she was leaving, he told her to stay on.

"We have some **unfinished business** to discuss," he said mysteriously.

"Unfinished business?" she laughed. He was such an exciting man. "I thought we'd both admitted that we're finished for this evening. Don't tell me you've found some reserve of energy from somewhere."

"Sit down, Toki." She dropped into the seat next to him, lit a cigarette, inhaled and began to blow rings into the air. He took the cigarette from her and stubbed it out in the ashtray.

"Listen, let's have a serious talk. You do know who I am, don't you?"

"Yes, of course," she said lazily, putting her head on his shoulder. "You're you."

"I'm **Diba Anang**, not 'Andy' as I told you the other day. Remember me? My uncle **Ewah** used to be cook to your family in **Apapa**."

"Diba Anang!" she exclaimed, jumping to her feet and staring at him. She felt weak at the knees as the past came rushing back to her. That crucial evening thirteen years before when she had had to admit to her parents that she was expecting a baby and that Diba was the father. The chaos that had followed and her **expulsion to the village**. The lie had saved her face at the time, but later she had been plagued by pangs of conscience as she dreaded ever meeting Diba again, and the accusations that would be sure to follow.

At the time she had had her family behind her and it had been her word against his; not that he had put up any defence whatsoever. What would happen now? Was he angry? He did not look it. It was as if he had a mask over his face. Would he beat her up in retribution? She hated violence. She took a few deep breaths to calm herself while she calculated the distance between her chair and the door. She could make a dash for it. But would that solve the problem? It was indeed a piece of unfinished business. She would have to be at her sweetest and try to persuade him to **forgive and forget**. That would pave the way for a better relationship between them. She sat down by him again and laid her hand on his knee.

"Diba, I'm very sorry for involving you in my misfortune so many years ago. At the time I was thoughtless and selfish and only wanted to save my neck, somehow, anyhow. You cannot imagine how much I suffered later thinking of the lie I had told and what you must have thought of me. I always dreaded meeting you again. I must say that I did not recognise you at all. You've changed a lot since our teenage years."

"Look, Toki, do you know you almost ruined my life?"

"In what way?" She was surprised to hear him talk with such bitterness. Sure, she had told a lie and put him in an awkward and embarrassing position at the time but she could not see in what way her action could have ruined his life. After all, no demands whatsoever had been made upon him.

"I was sent away by my uncle who was going to help me with my future plans. Due to your lie I could not carry out my intention of studying law at the university. You remember we both planned to read law?"

"I do. I'm so sorry my action affected your plans. Forgive me." She was indeed sorry, but still failed to see how his being sent away by his uncle had ruined his plans, unless of course the man had been going to finance his studies and had refused to do so because of the incident. Yet, if she could remember rightly, Diba's parents were better off than Ewah and he had gone back to them, according to reports. Had they refused to sponsor him? She tried to read what was going on in his mind.

"What beats me is why you picked me. Why didn't you involve one of the sons of your family friends with whom you were friendly? I'm surprised people believed your story."

"I'm sorry, Diba." Hell, she was getting fed-up with begging him for forgiveness. What did he want her to do?

"Maybe you thought that as a village boy, whose uncle was in your family's employ, I would not protest, and anyway, no one would believe what I said. Well, you thought right. **I was sent away without being listened to**. That's the power of position in our society." He laughed bitterly.

"I tried to trace you through your uncle some years afterwards so that I could apologise, but he was not forthcoming about your whereabouts and there was no one else I could ask. If I had recognised you that first day, I would probably have run away. That might have been better."

"No, that would not have helped," he said sadly. "Somehow, we would have met again somewhere." Suddenly, he felt his anger ebbing away, and he was thinking calmly. Had he actually suffered any real setback because of the girl's false accusation? His uncle had sent him away but he had parents who could have helped him if they had wanted to. He supposed his anger stemmed from the jealousy he felt that the girl had been able to realise her ambition despite all odds. He must not feel bitter that she had been luckier than he had been. Instead he should establish a good relationship between them so that she could be of help to him.

"All right, Toki," he said at length, patting the hand which lay on his knee, "**all is forgiven**. Let's forget about the whole thing and pretend we've just met. You're a sweet lady, you know, and I like you immensely."

She blushed and sighed inwardly. "Thank you, Diba."

After a short pause he asked, "Pardon

me, Toki, but I have a nagging question. Who was er, er, responsible for the pregnancy?" There was silence; then she began to sob. He regretted his question immediately. What did he want to know for? It was not his business. He hugged her and tried to soothe her.

"I'm sorry. I shouldn't have asked."

"Oh, no, you've a right to know," she said when she was calmer. "You more than anyone else. I had hoped that you'd not ask any further questions about the pregnancy, but now that you have, I'll tell you about it. You remember how strict my parents were about their children going to parties and mixing with the wrong sort of people?"

"Yes, of course."

"Well, there was this weekend that they were away in **Akure** for the chieftaincy ceremony of a friend. I was studying for my examinations and I could not go. You may also remember **Wunmi**, the flashy girl down the road, whom my parents forbade me to be friendly with?"

"I do. '**Miss High-life**' we used to call her."

"Yes. Well, I secretly admired her sophisticated ways and when she called that weekend to ask me to a party, I was only too eager to accept. I was flattered that she had sought out plain old me to accompany her. The party took place in a house in **Bamgbose Road**. At first it looked like an innocent teenage gathering. There were no alcoholic drinks or necking or any rough play. Soon I relaxed and began to enjoy myself chatting and dancing. When it began to get dark I signalled to Wunmi that it was time for me to leave. I had told my uncle, who was staying the weekend with us, that I was only going round to a friend's to borrow a book. She told me to hold on for some minutes while she said 'goodbye' to her friends.

Suddenly all the lights went out and some guests shouted 'NEPA', but no one made a move to leave. I noticed, however, that the record player was still on. It was not a power failure. I began to feel my way out. Mid-way hands grabbed me and I was dragged into another dark room and flung on to a bed. I struggled and screamed but my clothes were ripped off. You can imagine the rest of it. There must have been about four or five of them. At last I was left alone and I staggered out in my torn clothes into the street."

"What a terrible experience!"

"I was so filled with remorse and shame afterwards that for years I could not bear the touch of any man. It became a problem and I had to see a psychiatrist while studying abroad."

"Why didn't you go to the police? Those boys would have been arrested and charged in court."

"I could not go to the police without revealing that I had disobeyed my parents in the first place. Think of the scandal! What made it harder to bear was that there was no one to confide in. When I discovered that I was pregnant I almost took my own life, and it was only the vigilance of my mother that prevented this."

"Hm, anyway, I'm glad you got over it all. You got rid of the pregnancy and..."

"That's just it. I didn't."

"You mean there's a child?"

"Yes. My parents, who are staunch **Roman Catholics**, refused to hear about abortion."

"Where's the child now?"

"In a secondary school in Akure. He lives with my maternal aunt. He's twelve and in his first year. Quite a bright boy."

"Why doesn't he live with you?"

"I'm not married yet, so I can't have him stay with me. My parents do not want any mention made of him. I'm doing all I can for him considering the circumstances under which he was conceived."

She did not need to say any more. Diba had already realised that the boy was neither loved nor welcomed by members of his family. He felt sorry for him. What a life! Suddenly he felt angry.

"Why have you all rejected him? He did not ask to be born. You as his mother could at least show him some love and affection."

"I don't have to bend over backwards to please him or make him feel loved. I didn't ask him to come into the world either."

"That's a callous thing to say."

"I'm being truthful. He's quite happy. I sent him to the best private primary school I could afford and he doesn't lack for food or good clothes."

"What about motherly love?"

"He wouldn't have everything even if he had both his parents to look after him. As it is, I don't know who the father is. I didn't see the faces of those boys. Look, Diba, it's a terribly depressing topic for me."

"I'm sorry. It's just that I know what it is to be unloved by the family."

"Don't worry about **Etim**, he's..."

"Etim? Is that his name? You gave him a **Cross River** name?"

"That was the name your uncle gave him."

"You mean you never told the truth about his conception?"

"No, not even to my parents. You're the first to know."

"Really? So, you carried the farce further by giving him my name. His surname is **'Anang'**, isn't it?"

"Yes." She looked at him anxiously. "Diba, please consider it a coincidence that you both have the same surname. He's not your child and there's no question of any demand being made on you. I could make a signed declaration to that effect if you are worried."

"No, that does not bother me. I would like to meet Etim. What have you told him about his father? That he is dead?"

"That idea did occur to me, but since your uncle and my family believed that he was your son and there'd been no news of your death, I could not tell him that. He believes that his father is a **seafarer** who hardly ever comes home."

"Hard to swallow."

"He used to ask about his father's relatives, but when he sensed that I was not anxious to discuss them, he dropped the topic. Besides, I don't see him frequently. He spends all his holidays with my aunt."

"Toki, do me a favour. Invite him to Lagos for his next holiday."

"Where will he stay? I can't..."

"He'll stay with me. I'll play uncle to him."

"No, no charity, please. He's perfectly well-adjusted as he is."

"Sshh, Toki. If my uncle made him an 'Anang', then he's one. After all, according to you, most of those who know about him think he's my child."

She reflected for a while. She did not

want the child with her, but it might not be a bad thing if he was introduced to a member of his 'father's' family. He needed to have a family tie somewhere. Would Diba be able to keep up the pretence forever?

"My only fear is that he might become emotionally disturbed if he is told later that...?"

"No fear of that, Toki. I give you my word that I will always remain a member of my family. I never go back on my word. He's my nephew."

The next school holiday came and went without Toki asking Etim to come. She offered no explanation and Diba refrained from saying anything about it although their friendship grew steadily and they saw each other frequently.

He introduced her to the **Oligas** who received her warily at first, but when they noticed that she was not possessive about him, she was put on their invitation list. Mrs. Oliga liked asking her advice on certain matters pertaining to her business even though she had her own lawyer. Ebi, who wouldn't serve the girls Diba usually brought to parties there with food and drinks, went out of her way to be nice to Toki.

Diba profited a great deal from their relationship. Many doors which otherwise would have remained shut to him opened as he accompanied her to important parties. Sometimes he wondered what these people would do if they knew they were hobnobbing with a man convicted of **armed robbery**. That conviction hung over him like a dark cloud. A plan formed in his mind.

At the end of a lovely weekend which they had spent together in **Tarkwa Bay** he told her a friend of his needed her advice. This friend had been wrongfully convicted of armed robbery and, although he had served his term and been released, he wanted to know if there was anything he could do to prove his innocence.

Toki said that the only thing she could think of was to ask a state counsel friend of hers to look in the **High Court archives** for the aftermath of the conviction—whether someone else had confessed to that particular offence or not. He gave her the relevant names and dates, being careful that she should not associate him with the '**Andy Brown**' in the case, and some weeks later she told him that she had news for him.

"I could do with some good news," he said.

"It's about your friend."

"Oh, yes."

"A few years after his conviction a group of armed robbers about to be executed said they had been responsible for that robbery. They took the police to where they had abandoned the stolen **taxi cab** in the bush off **Ikorodu Road**. The unfortunate thing about the case was that before your friend could be contacted at **Damay Prison** and arrangements made for his release he had been transferred to a prison in another part of the country following his participation in a **prison riot**."

"Hm, I didn't know about that," Diba

lied.

He wondered if Toki's friend had given a full description of 'Andy Brown'. She was a pretty smart lady and might try to find out who the convicted person really was. Maybe he ought not to have told her about the incident at all. But he needed to clear his name for the peace of his own mind and for the future. If he could confidently quote where his case could be found in the court archives, then he could prove, to anyone who wanted to know, that he had been wrongfully convicted.

"Thank you very much, darling Tokunboh," he said, kissing her. "If you'll give me details of where reference was made to this case, then I can pass them on to my friend. He'll be so relieved."

"Glad to be of help. Here, I've written everything down. However, my advice is that your friend should not reopen the case. The judge and most of those concerned are dead. It's a pity he could not be traced after the riot otherwise he would have been out earlier."

"Well, that was just his luck. He'll have to accept that."

Two months later Diba asked Toki to marry him. He was not in love with her but liked her a lot and knew that being married to her would bring many advantages. She was popular and he would shoot up the social ladder. This would help him in the business he hoped to establish. It sounded calculating but people have been known to marry for worse reasons.

"I'm fond of you Diba," she told him, "but marriage with you will not work."

"Why not?"

"Because your style is different from mine. You're too intense and take life too seriously. You would make too many demands on me and I would not be able to live up to your expectations. You'd be disappointed and I'd be frustrated."

"If we know all these pitfalls we could avoid them."

"No, I don't want to go through life

treading carefully all the time. I want to be me and live life to the full the way I know how to. Now, **my old man** is more my type of guy. Apart from the fact that we love each other he's the only man I know who can put up with my whims and caprices. Many people believe it's his money I'm after, but it isn't and he knows it. That's why he's asked me to marry him."

"Are you going to?"

"Oh yes. As soon as certain formalities have been completed, I'll stop seeing you, you gorgeous chap, and get married to him."

"That'll kill me."

"No, it won't. It will leave you free for the woman you love."

"The woman I love? Who is she?"

"That'd be telling! It's so obvious I noticed it the day you introduced me to her."

Toki was so sharp! Marriage to her would not have worked. He wanted a home-loving, warm and sympathetic lady for a partner. Someone who was on the same wavelength as he was, who would give him all the love and care that had eluded him all these years. Toki was nice and elegant but totally selfish. He would miss her when she got married. She was such good fun.

CHAPTER 7

It was a few days before **Christmas** and Diba was putting up decorations and thinking about what his **New Year resolutions** were going to be, when there was a ring at the door.

"Hi," greeted Toki. With her was a sullen-looking and busy boy of about thirteen. For once she seemed nervous and unsure of herself as she introduced him.

"Diba, this is Etim. Etim, this is the uncle I told you about, who had kindly invited you over to spend the Christmas holiday with him. Diba, I'm sorry I could not inform you earlier about the exact date of his arrival, but I know that you'll understand..."

"Perfectly, Toki. Etim's always welcome here. He's my nephew; I don't need to make elaborate preparations for his visit."

"Thank you. Er, if you two don't mind, I'll just disappear. I have to see the doctor." With a quick wave at them both, Tokunboh got into her car and drove off.

Diba smiled. How like Toki to avoid any embarrassing situation. If he knew her, she would not call at his flat again until the boy's holiday was almost over. She would have a good excuse too. She had just got married and was **three months pregnant**. He wished she had given him some warning, but this was typical of Tokunboh's impulsiveness.

"Come in, Etim," he said to the boy who stood staring at him. "This is your room. Unpack your suitcase and come and help with the decorations. You kids usually have such bright ideas about where to hang up what. Have you had lunch?"

"I'm not hungry," said the boy rudely. Diba looked at him briefly but said nothing. Two hours later, Etim had still not come out of his room. Diba looked in. He was lying on the bed staring at the ceiling. His suitcase remained unopened on the floor.

"What's the matter, Etim? Are you sick?"

"No."

"Tired?"

"No."

"Don't you want to unpack your things?" There was no response.

"Are you unhappy about coming here?" The boy shrugged his shoulders indifferently, making no attempt to get up. If there was anything that made Diba mad, it was insolence from children.

"Get up, Etim, and get this straight," he said sternly. "Come on, get up," he repeated, advancing towards the bed as Etim hesitated, and then got up. "Now, I felt it was time you met members of your father's family after all these years, and that was why I invited you here. I know what you must feel about being abandoned by the Anang family and I sympathise, but one day, when you're older and more fully integrated in the family circle, you'll feel better and your past resentment will be forgotten. You're still very young but you must make the effort now to start making new acquaintances." Diba was not actually angry, but he knew he had to pull Etim out of his mood, for his own good. He was really anxious to play uncle to him and make him feel he belonged somewhere. Etim hung his head sullenly and would say nothing. Diba began to get impatient.

"Do I take it that you do not want to meet your father's relations?"

Silence.

"All right," said Diba, picking up the suitcase, "I'll return you to your mother. I like you and have been looking forward to becoming friends with you, but it seems as if you don't care at all. Let's go."

"Oh, no, no, sir," cried the boy, going to him and taking the suitcase from him. "Please, sir, don't send me away."

"Uncle," corrected Diba.

"I mean, Uncle. I would like to stay."

"I would like you to stay, too." He laid a hand on the boy's shoulder. "But why the sullenness?"

"It's because, Auntie, I mean, er, my mother, told me only this morning when I arrived that I was going to my paternal uncle's. When she wrote to say I could come and spend this holiday in Lagos, I thought it would be with her. It would have been the first time, but..." He broke off, on the verge of tears. Diba felt close to tears too, but decided to make light of the situation.

"Never mind that now, my boy. Your mother has just got married and should be given time to settle down. Besides, what fun would it be, staying with a lady?" He feigned scorn. "But you'll have lots of fun with me because we're both men and can be up to all sorts of things together. Come on, boy, let's get something to eat. Can you cook?"

"Yes, Uncle," Etim answered, brightening up. "Where's the kitchen? What would you like to have? I'm hungry too." Like any child, he was beginning to forget his self-pity and look forward to an exciting holiday with his unknown uncle.

Soon the holiday was over and it was time for Etim to go back to Akure. He had had such a nice time that, already, he had asked to be allowed to come back.

"You're always welcome here, Etim. I hope you realise that," said Diba gently. He had enjoyed the holiday too. It was the first time he had looked after a teenager and, although it had not been easy, he had enjoyed having someone to look after. He found his 'nephew' restless and inquisitive. He wanted to know all about his father and his people. Diba had to go carefully on this and he spoke generally about the family and customs in the Cross River State. One day, he promised, he would tell Etim about his father. He would have to consult Toki first, he told himself. Etim certainly needed stern handling for he was stubborn and used to having his own way. He and Diba had had a few brushes, but Diba had gently but firmly told the boy that he could not have his own way all the time. He would have to take other people's feelings and points of view into consideration. By the time the holiday was over, they both understood each other well.

Diba had introduced him to the Oligas and Etim was warmly welcomed by Mrs. Oliga in particular, who was glad to meet someone from Diba's family at last and to learn a little bit more about him. When she was told that Toki was the mother, she concluded at once that Diba must be the father and not the uncle, but she kept this to herself. Somehow the knowledge raised her esteem for him because she felt that if he had had such an intimate relationship with someone with a reputable family background, like Toki, he must have had good connections too.

Diba was extremely happy when he was offered the position of **Banquet Manager** with the **Port Harcourt** branch of the **Riverine Hotels**. He was to be on attachment with the Head Office for three months before moving to Port Harcourt. His dreams were gradually coming true.

Although Mrs. Oliga, as his employer, had given him a good recommendation for the job, he felt he deserved to get it on his qualifications and experience, but his ego was somewhat deflated when he glanced at the foot of the letter from the company and found that Mrs. Oliga was one of its directors. Had she had a say in his appointment? He would not want that.

"No, Diba," she told him when he asked her about it. "I wouldn't do such a thing. I didn't know there was such a vacancy going until you asked me to give you a reference. No one contacted me. I'm sure you got the job entirely on your own merits. Are you satisfied?"

"I am. You've done so much for me already, but I very much want to see how other people react to my capabilities. I would hate to be propped up all my life."

"Personally, I think you will be an asset to any organisation you work for. You're a loyal and a dedicated worker. My first reaction when you asked for a reference was to give you such a lousy one that no one would ever think of employing you, so you'd always be here with me." She laughed. "That would have been selfish I suppose. Oh, I'll miss you so much, Diba."

"I'll miss you too, but you must understand the need for me to strike out on my own and be nearer home."

"Yes, of course, I understand."

Diba had become so fond of Etim that he was determined to move him to a school in **Cross River State** so that they could be near each other. Toki had no objection. She'd had her baby and was very busy looking after him, and holding down a job. When Diba spoke of adopting Etim, however, she was against the idea.

"You don't have to, you know. It's enough that you're playing 'uncle'. He should be quite satisfied with that."

"But I'm not. I love him and want him as a son. In fact, I don't even have to adopt him. He's my son. I'll tell him when next I see him that I'm his real father and that you and I could not get married when he was conceived because we were too young. I hope you don't mind."

"I do, very much." Diba was surprised.

"Why? You don't want him. I know you've catered for most of his needs but you must admit you've no room in your heart for him."

"That's what you think. Anyway, I'm his mother and I have the right to decide who his father is."

"I see. Well, who is the father?"

"Er, er, that's not your business." She could not say why she was trying to put a spanner in the works. She ought to be pleased at this new development, at least for the boy's sake, but she felt she might be totally cut off from him if Diba declared himself the father.

"I'm sorry, Toki," said Diba, cutting into her thoughts, "it's my business. You're just being selfish and unreasonable. You really don't care one way or the other about him. I have a sneaking suspicion you don't want him to be happy. Somehow you want him to pay for your own foolishness."

"That's not true. What happened wasn't my fault."

"Whose fault was it? Yours, I'm afraid."

"In what way?"

"If you had told your parents the truth about his conception, religion or no religion, they would have agreed to the termination of the pregnancy since your life was not in any danger. For no one wants to bring a child into the world whose mother has been the object of **rape by several unknown persons**. That would be giving the child a bad start in life." He hated talking to her like that but, since she was being disagreeable, he felt the truth must be brought home to her to force her hand.

Toki did not like the turn the discussion was taking. It confused and embarrassed her.

"However you go on," she persisted, "I won't allow you to be the father."

"You have no choice. On the birth certificate it says 'the son of **Tokunboh Laja and Diba Anang**'. I have it in my possession. As a lawyer you should know that you wouldn't have a leg to stand on if you took me to court over the matter. There'd be a great scandal which would rock your family. I have nothing to lose. A blood test might even show that I could be Etim's father. You never can tell."

Toki bowed her head. "All right, have it your way. But from now, you'll assume full responsibility for him since that's what you want."

"It is indeed. Relax Toki. My decision is in the best interests of everybody. You'll see."

On her way out she paused at the door, then ran back to him and flung her arms around his neck, crying. "Thank you ever so much, Diba. You're a very good friend and a fine gentleman. Don't take any notice of my pigheadedness. I'm very grateful for all you've done for Etim and me. May God bless and reward you. Bring Etim up the way you like. Even though you're not really his father, I have full confidence in your ability to play that role successfully." With that she left.

Etim was extremely delighted at the news. He said that he had already suspected that Diba was his real father. Diba prayed silently that he would not let anyone down in his new role.

CHAPTER 8

Diba did not find his new job much fun. The attachment was useful and he learned fast but the Banquet Manager at Head Office, a lady, was a difficult person to work with. She tried to do the jobs of her two assistants as well as her own. She took every order that came in, if possible, and she made sure that she was the only one who contacted the other sectional heads in the hotel. The result was steady chaos as orders and instructions were forgotten and things had to be sorted out at the last minute. The responsibility for doing this was shoved on to the assistants who were accused of incompetence. Diba was glad that he was not going to be based there as he would not have been able to resist having a shouting match with her. He marvelled at how stoically **Mr. Ossom**, one of her deputies, took it all. He was always unruffled and he would smilingly sort out the mess.

"It's nothing," he said, shrugging his shoulders. "I'm used to it. She's nice really, but she's got marital problems and her job is all she has, so she guards it jealously."

"If her job means so much to her, then she should do it well. She hardly ever delegates and she can't cope with all the duties in her department. What does she have deputies for? Don't the authorities know what's going on?"

"Management knows all right but she has always been quite competent in the past; besides her uncle is **Chairman of the Board**, so there's really nothing anyone can do as of now."

"Hm! That's a pity. She's heading for a breakdown the way she's driving herself."

"Yes. Well, she's had one before and virtually lives on 'pick-me-ups' in the mornings, and 'slow-me-downs' at night."

Diba missed his old job where he was trusted so much even though he had been working practically off his feet. He spent his idle hours on this one dreaming about his new station in life. A fully-furnished house and a car went with the position. He was full of suppressed excitement as he thought of the life ahead.

He was half dozing in a chair while listening to a quiz programme on the radio one Friday afternoon when a car screeched to a halt outside. He woke up and went to the window. An elegantly dressed young lady in a long, tight-fitting skirt and a **halter top** made from lace came down from a brand new **Japanese car**. She wore high heeled shoes and a pair of sophisticated sunglasses. She locked up the car and tried to walk briskly towards the block of flats. Her contours struggled within her tight clothes but she managed somehow. Diba watched her progress with interest, admiring the neat, short **hair-do** and shapely figure. Who was she calling on? Half-way, she stopped as if in thought and looked up at Diba's window. He withdrew quickly.

"Phew!" It was **Ebi**. She was unrecognisable in that outfit. She had always seemed to live in her uniform or slacks. She looked so mature and seductive that afternoon! Was she calling on him? She had been there several times of course, but only in the company of her mother or her brothers. And the car! Surely she did not own one? Diba ran a comb through his hair and quickly spruced up his sitting room. The doorbell went. He allowed it to ring twice more and then went to open the door. He feigned surprise at seeing her.

"Why, hello Ebi. This is a lovely surprise!"

"Hello, Diba," she said, shyly fiddling with her keys.

"Come in," he invited, stepping aside for her. She hesitated, then walked in stiffly.

"Won't you sit down? I don't bite!" As Ebi complied, Diba continued, "Can I get you a drink?"

"Er, no, thank you."

"Why?"

"Er, I don't feel like drinking."

"Oh, I see." He asked after her family and waited for her to get to the object of her visit. Perhaps she had a message from her mother? An invitation to a party or perhaps an assignment for him to carry out? She had never before called on him on her own for, although she now behaved more civilly towards him, they were still far from being real friends.

He asked after **Tamu**. She answered briefly. Silence. She kept twisting and untwisting the handkerchief in her hand. He got up and put on the television. Her attitude was gradually getting on his nerves. Had she come to stare at him? Or accuse him of something? Or perhaps to apologise for her past behaviour?

"Well, Ebi, it's nice of you to call to see 'old Uncle Diba', but if you're going to sit there as if in a trance, and refuse a drink, perhaps you could tell me why you decided to honour me with your lovely presence." It was not the most polite thing to say, but anything to prod her tongue into action was worth trying.

Diba was totally unprepared for what happened next. Ebi burst into tears and rushed towards the door. He caught up with her on the stairs and coaxed her back into his flat. He showed her into the bathroom so that she could recover and wash her face. When she came back to the sitting room, he sat her in a chair and made her sip some **brandy**.

"Now, Ebi," he said gently, sitting himself down next to her. **"Tell me what the matter is. Are you in trouble?"** Flashes of what had happened to Toki in their teenage years came to his mind. Was Ebi in the family way? Damn it, she couldn't be, and even if she were, her mother would be the first person she would confide in. They were quite close. Besides she was no ignorant school girl, and would surely not allow herself to be taken unawares.

"Trouble?" she echoed, looking at him in faint surprise. This aroused his impatience.

"I mean what's the drama all about?"

"Drama?" asked Ebi, a bit foolishly.

"Hell!" Diba got up and began to pace the room. Really! Really! The girl made him so mad! "What do you want here for Christ's sake?" he burst out.

Ebi began to sob again. She got up, stumbling towards the door. Diba barred her way, determined to get to the root of the matter.

"Ebi, for goodness' sake, pull yourself together." He sat her down in a straight-backed chair this time and pulled one out for himself. "You're a **nurse**, remember? You're not expected to go to pieces like this. What is it?" he continued, a bit more gently.

Ebi turned away from him. "You don't like me," she burst out. "In fact, you hate me and..."

"Hear who's talking about dislike," he wanted to tease her, but he held his tongue. The poor girl looked miserable enough already.

"I don't dislike you, Ebi. You don't understand me at all."

"I, I, came to show you my car and you didn't even congratulate me; you pretended you didn't see it."

"Your car? Have you bought a car? No one told me about it."

"It was delivered only this afternoon." They both went to the window. Diba was effusive in his congratulations.

"Ebi, this is wonderful. Simply fantastic. Congratulations!"

Ebi smiled and shook his hand. "I came straight here to show it to you. Mother hasn't seen it yet. I wanted you to be the first to congratulate me."

That startled him. "Why?" he asked in confusion.

"Because I, I, well, I think of you constantly and I..." Was it possible that she cared as much as he did? He had fallen deeply in love with her as he recovered from his illness when he was living with her family. It had been a ridiculous situation then for the more rudely and indifferently she had treated him the more deeply in love he had fallen. It had taken all his courage to conceal his feelings and feign indifference. He had been jealous of her boyfriends and would wait up each night she was out.

"Ebi," he said softly, "come to me." She went to him and he folded her in his arms. They swayed a bit as if in a dream.

"Did you really think I was out to defraud your family?" he asked her some time later.

"No, I didn't think so. I knew you were quite loyal to Mother, but I didn't want to believe it and I looked for ways of proving to her that she should not have so much confidence in you."

"But why? I was not trying to displace either you or your brothers in her affections. She was my benefactor and I was only showing my gratitude."

"I guess I was consumed with jealousy at the apparent closeness between the two of you. I must confess that I realised I was in love with you only after you had moved out."

"Oh, my darling," he said, kissing her. "And I thought you didn't care."

"I thought I would be happy when you left, but I wasn't. Instead I kept thinking of you, and I could have killed those girls you brought to our place. I kept away for so long because I felt you must hate me for the way I treated you. Today, however, I had to take my courage in both hands and come to you. I wanted you to share my happiness."

"Bless you, sweetheart," he said tenderly. "That makes me feel really good. Ebi, it's as if I'm dreaming."

"I feel that way too. It's as if it will soon be morning and I will wake up to find it has all been a dream." They gazed lovingly into each other's eyes.

"Come, my love," he said, pulling her into his arms again. "Let me show you it's no dream, and also make sure that you don't disappear." She nestled against him. Then a thought hit her.

"Diba, are you and Mother still er, er, um..."

"Yes, darling? Are we still what?"

"Er, er, lovers," she blurted out, quickly looking away.

"Lovers!" he exclaimed, looking at her in wonder. "Your mother and I are lovers! Who said we were?"

"Well," she said, feeling very embarrassed, "no one really, but you both behaved as if you were. At least, I had that impression."

"How could you have? Did you see us kissing, holding hands, making love?"

"Er, no, but..."

"Look, if your mother patted my chin or hugged me when I had performed a satisfactory assignment for her, then it was a brotherly gesture which, as I'm sure you're aware, it is part of the **African culture**. People embrace all the time. Your mother and Tamu do it."

"Yes, but..."

"Who else thought your mother was my mistress? Tamu and your brothers?"

"I don't know. Maybe I was just jealous."

"I'm sure your mother would be horrified to know that you regarded our relationship that way. No wonder you have been so suspicious of me. A penniless young man worming himself into the affections of a wealthy woman; perhaps marrying her secretly and disinheriting her children!"

Ebi mumbled something. She felt ashamed because those had been precisely her thoughts. She also felt glad that Diba had never been in love with anyone else. He was solely hers. She smiled at him and moved closer. He held her tightly.

He went on, half seriously now. "I respect and admire your mother as I would anyone who's as helpful and kind as she is, but to become her lover and under her own roof? Never! And in the circumstances under which I came to her? I have some pride left! Apart from the age-gap you had already captured my heart so there was no room for anyone else." Ebi was filled with ecstasy.

They went outside with a bottle of wine and christened the car. Then Diba drove it around for a while.

Diba now realised he was no longer looking forward to his transfer to **Port Harcourt**. He discussed his appointment with Ebi and was pleasantly surprised when she told him that she would resign from her job and go to work there too so as to be near him. He proposed to her that evening and was accepted.

So much for his desire to stay away from **Flint**! How could he do that now that he was going to marry his **cousin**? But he was so wildly in love that the problem no longer assumed the importance it had before. Even Flint would not want to involve him in criminal activities if he found him respectably married. What really mattered was that Ebi did not think that he was after the money she was likely to inherit from her mother.

Mrs. Oliga obviously thought otherwise. She absolutely refused to allow the marriage. She stormed round to Diba's place dragging poor Tamu along. She refused to answer his polite "Good afternoon, Auntie."

"Don't you 'Auntie' me! Tell me. Is it true that you proposed to Ebi and she accepted your offer of marriage?"

"Yes."

"I see. Well, I refuse to give my consent. The whole thing is ridiculous."

"Why, Auntie? Do you feel we are not old and responsible enough to marry or that we are not sufficiently fond of each other to do so?"

"Don't ask me questions. Just listen. I forbid you to see Ebi any more."

"What does she say about that?"

"That's not your business. Just do as you are told."

"I'm afraid I can't stop seeing her unless she tells me to. We are two responsible adults who know what they are about."

"I don't think you do. Look, Diba," she said, standing over him, her hands on her hips, "after all I've done for you, are you trying to disobey me?"

"I'm afraid so, yes. I'm extremely grateful to you for what you did for me, but I love Ebi and she loves me. Until she tells me to stop, I shall continue seeing her."

"Really? Hm! I can't believe it. You refuse to do my bidding! You, whom I rescued from the gutter and made into a man. You came to me a trembling wretch and I..." Diba bit his lip to control his anger.

"Caro," said Tamu, getting up, "let's go. You're going too far. Leave the boy alone. I'm sure he'll change his decision."

"Thank you, sir. It's Ebi's attitude that will determine that."

"You're a **fortune hunter**," said Mrs. Oliga desperately. "You think you can lay your greedy hands on my money by marrying my daughter, you scheming so-and-so."

"I refuse to believe that you actually think that," said Diba, getting up. "You know in your heart that the allegation is wrong. I'll sign an undertaking, if you like, renouncing any right to Ebi's money when we are married. For our children too. So, any money that's Ebi's, that is, if she accepts money from you after all this, will not be brought into our home. I think I am perfectly capable of fending for my wife and children."

"I see. We'll see about this marriage of yours. You haven't heard the last of me yet. Prepare for war."

"Come, Caro, let's go," said Tamu, leading her away. Diba hoped Ebi would take a firm, positive stand on the issue. Surely, she would not be intimidated by threats of disinheritance from her mother? She would be sufficiently fond of him to withstand parental wrath.

"Caro," said Tamu to Mrs. Oliga on their way home, "I think you went too far in accusing Diba. No man would tolerate that. What have you against him apart from not knowing much about him?"

"Isn't that grounds enough for objecting to the marriage?"

"He might make a good husband for Ebi. You know how much in love they are. You were the first to notice it while he was still living with you."

"I know. I like Diba very much and I had to work very hard at being angry with him. I said several hurtful things to him which I knew were not true, but the relationship has to be broken up. Ebi has refused to listen to me. He has too. Now, what do I do?"

"Leave them. When he moves to Port Harcourt, they'll see less of each other and the relationship will die a natural death."

"It won't. Ebi has put in a letter of resignation at the hospital and she has written to my brother to help her look for a job in Port Harcourt."

"Is that so? Hm! these young people!" Tamu chuckled to himself as he thought back to his own days of courtship.

"There's nothing to laugh about," she said, frowning.

"I know what I'll do. I'll tell Ebi the truth about her..."

"Why?" exclaimed Tamu, shocked. "I thought it was agreed years ago that there would never be any need for that."

"There is now, since the girl is being extremely stubborn. I'll tell her the truth and that should end any further talk of marriage to Diba. I would hate to see what happened to me happen to her too."

"But Diba is different from..."

"You don't really know, do you? The most charming person may also be the most devilish. Let her marry **Princewill** as she had planned to do before Diba came along. He's a nice, good-looking boy whose family is well-known in Cross River State."

"Perhaps Ebi prefers a man with a mystery

surrounding him. A dark horse. Ha! Ha!"

"Tamu," she said reproachfully, "you're treating the whole thing like a huge joke. I want a peaceful old age, free from worries, if I can."

"Everyone wants that. But Caro, marriage is a very tricky thing. There's no guarantee for happiness. A partner's attitude can change at any time. Look, emulate my relaxed attitude towards my children. I said, 'Righto' to any partner they brought home, and prayed that they'd be able to bear whatever the outcome of the union might be. In Ebi's case, there's no cause for alarm. She has a profession and she's a very independent person, like you, who can look after herself."

Diba was very hurt and disappointed when Ebi tearfully told him that she could no longer marry him because of what her mother had just revealed to her. What hurt him most was that she refused to confide in him.

"If you loved me," he accused, "you

would tell me what the matter was. Are you sworn to secrecy over it?"

"No. If I told you, you would lose all respect for me and would not want to be associated with me."

"Why not try me? Was it something you did in the past?"

"No, I knew nothing about it and couldn't have helped it anyway. No one could have. Fate just thrust it upon us." She began to sob.

Diba did not know what to say. What could have happened? Had it anything to do with Flint? In what way would it affect their marriage?

"Why should whatever it is affect our marriage since it has nothing to do with your own personal experience?"

"I've just told you. You'd despise me."

"Why should I? There's always a secret or two in every family. I love you and it's our reaction to each other that should matter. You don't really love me, Ebi. Maybe you wanted me because you wanted to triumph over your mother by taking her supposed lover."

"That's a very hurtful thing to say, Diba, and you know it isn't true. I love you with all my heart, but I cannot live happily with you knowing that you're trying hard to conceal your contempt for me and my family. With a man with fewer scruples, it would be easy. He would shrug off everything. But I've studied you carefully and I know that you have high morals."

"Has it anything to do with **birth legitimacy**? I already have a son after all, and it doesn't matter in the least if..."

"No, it isn't that at all. That sort of thing is no handicap in our society these days. Diba, see, I'll take my broken heart away and devote the rest of my life to my work."

"You're over-dramatising and behaving like a martyr. Are you the only one affected? Damn it, my own heart is broken too, and through no fault of mine."

CHAPTER 9

A week later Diba and Etim moved to **Port Harcourt**. The hotel was situated on the outskirts of the town on the road to the **International Airport**. He was given a bungalow in the staff quarters and he got Etim into one of the local secondary schools. He missed Ebi very much but was pleased to be away from the hectic life of **Lagos**.

Here, things were on a much lower key and more peaceful. It was nice to wake up in the morning and have the time to watch the birds, jog for a while in the garden, have a leisurely bath and breakfast and finally walk to the office. In the evening, he tended the garden, read or strolled to a nearby fishing village where he had made some friends. For the first time in years he felt close to nature.

His job was challenging and satisfying although not without its **teething problems**.

He had staff who wanted to get paid for doing nothing. His predecessor, who had retired, had been an easy-going man who left the workers alone when they did not feel the urge to work. Diba was not going to stand for that, but he was careful how he threw his weight around because the **workers' union** there was strong. He spoke persuasively to the leaders, pointing out to them that it was in the interest of all that every worker should do his job well, and be punctual and regular at work, otherwise if they lost their customers to the other international hotels in Port Harcourt, they would all be out of work. A responsible man, he told them, should earn his salary. After a few brushes here and there, the people in his department understood the sort of man he was and settled down to their duties.

The cocktail party to mark the end of the annual meeting of the country's **Commissioners for Agriculture** was under way and Diba looked in to make sure that everything was in order. He usually did this whenever the hotel was hosting any big event. The **General Manager** had always impressed on his managers that a contented customer would always want to come back and that no effort should be spared to give a good and satisfying service. Diba always bore this in mind. Besides, the **State Government** was an important customer.

"And now, ladies and gentlemen," the master-of-ceremony for the occasion was saying, "I'll call on the Commissioner of Agriculture from the Cross River State to give the vote of thanks. **Chief Joseph Anang**!" On hearing the name, Diba was startled, and he strained his neck to see better. A tall, thin, middle-aged man in glasses went to the microphone. It was **Joe**, his eldest brother! He could hardly keep still as he watched. Home seemed nearer. Although there was a difference of about fifteen years between them, they had been very close in the family. That was until that unfortunate afternoon when the wrist watch of Joe's bride had been found with Diba. It had been a terrible day: everyone had descended on him and his mother had collapsed from the humiliation of it all and been ill for several days. Joe had never forgiven him and things had never been the same between them again. Diba remembered all these things as he tried to recall when he had last seen his brother. His enthusiasm was not dampened however by the past. He made enquiries and was told that Joe was staying at the **Seven Feathers Hotel**.

"Joe, this is your kid brother, Diba. I'm speaking from the reception of your hotel." He smiled as he heard an audible intake of breath followed by an exclamation.

"Good evening, sir. This is Chief Joseph Anang. Please could you repeat what you've just said?"

Diba did so.

"Did you say Diba? Diba, my little brother?"

"Yes, Joe."

"Look, come right up. I'm in Room 510. No, I can't wait. Stay there. I'll come right down. Now where's my shirt and..." Diba could imagine the commotion going on as

Joe got ready. He had always been a little bit disorganised.

The meeting in the lobby was very emotional as they embraced over and over again. They went up to Joe's room and Diba asked for news of the family. Their parents were still alive and leading the same life as before. They had all been very worried when **Ewah** had written to say that Diba had disappeared after putting a girl in the family way. Joe and their mother had travelled down to Lagos to look for him. There had been a terrible family row in which the blame had been put squarely at Ewah's door. How could he have callously sent his nephew away like that? He should have brought him back home. Diba opened his mouth to protest for he had seen the letter written by their father in which he had said that Ewah could send him away if he liked. But he shut his mouth again. What was the point of reopening old wounds? The earlier they all forgot about that period of their lives the better. So he murmured something and changed the subject.

Joe was very glad to know that Diba was doing well. They arranged to meet at his house in **Calabar** that weekend so that they could go to **Ukum** together. Diba took Etim along. They had become so attached to each other that the roles of father and son came naturally.

The village had developed into a small town which was linked to several big villages by two busy major roads. Modern buildings stood side by side with the traditional ones in the various compounds. Some of them would be vacant for most of the year as their owners resided in the cities and visited only during the festive occasions. Diba had left during the **military regime** when the presence of soldiers had been felt everywhere; now he could see signs pointing to the local headquarters of the various political parties. The children had become more **sophisticated** too. There were no naked ones and they no longer ran out to wave at the odd car passing through the village. There was a **petrol station** and at least one vehicle in every street. As they passed by the local **comprehensive school**, he thought of his own school days—they had been terrible, full of beatings and accusations!

A cry went up as soon as Joe's car pulled up at the gate of the **Anang compound**. He had sent word ahead and they were eagerly expected. Diba's parents could hardly speak as they embraced him and wept openly. Everyone was in a joyous mood. Large quantities of food and drink had been provided and it was an **open house** to neighbours and any passer-by who cared to join them.

"The return of the **prodigal son**," thought Diba with a wry smile. Joe, of course, had not failed to mention in the note he had sent ahead that Diba was the **Banquet Manager** of the famous **Riverine Hotel** in Port Harcourt. So women at the gathering talked about how lucky **Mrs. Anang** was to have a Chief and a Commissioner, and now a Manager amongst her children. Some business-minded farmers amongst the guests had already hinted to Diba that they would like to supply his hotel with foodstuffs. Others wanted him to help find employment for their children or relatives. Everyone seemed keen on making his acquaintance so as to get one favour or the other done. He ran out of **visiting cards** within one hour. He was disgusted. Did anyone there really care about him? If he had come back a failure and in rags would he have got this rousing reception? He felt like mounting a rostrum and telling them all in a loud voice that he had served a term as an armed robber. There would be silence and the guests would slip away quietly. His parents would probably die from shame. That was the way of the world.

"Diba, my son," his mother told him that night, "congratulations on having such a lovely son as Etim. I'm glad that you accepted your responsibility as a man and decided to bring him up yourself. He must come here for his holidays so that he can learn to speak our language and get to know his cousins. Meanwhile I think you ought to take a wife. Is there anyone special you want to marry or can we look around here for a nice girl for you?"

"Mama, there was someone special, but she jilted me for some reasons she would not disclose. You can look for a girl for me. I'm not fussy about age, colour, religion or size," he added humorously, "but she must be a good home maker."

He had been thinking hard about marriage for some time now and had decided that, since Ebi would not marry him, he would marry any nice girl who came along.

Idia was a plump, lovely, dark-skinned Ukum girl who was in her final year in a **teachers' training college** in Calabar. Diba liked her at once. She was warm and exuded charm and was considered one of the best girls around. Both families agreed to the match and after all the formalities about the **traditional wedding** had been completed, Diba went back to Port Harcourt. Idia was to join him on the completion of her course.

A week before her arrival, Diba had a visitor in his office—a tall, good-looking boy in his early twenties. There was a whiff of **whisky** in the air when he spoke.

"I brought you this letter," he said. "It's from Idia."

Diba smiled as he opened it. "Please sit down," he said.

"No, I'll be leaving shortly." The boy began to pace the room.

Diba finished reading the note and looked up. He tried to assemble his thoughts. This was totally unexpected.

"You're **Cliff**?"

The other nodded.

"Idia says here that she cannot marry me because you're both very much in love and have always meant to get married after your graduation from college."

"Yeah," said the boy with a drawl. He was trying hard to conceal his nervousness. Diba felt sorry for him; he must have taken some whisky to fortify himself for the ordeal ahead.

"That was before you came along and her people felt she was better off marrying a Manager. She doesn't love you. She just got carried along, but now she's realised that she cannot live without me," he added triumphantly.

"Congratulations," Diba said drily. "But why couldn't she come and tell me all this herself? Was she afraid?"

"Oh no, not at all. She thought, well, we decided that I should bring the note. She's waiting in a taxi outside."

"I'd like to see her, then." Diba got up, but sat down again. "On second thoughts, I'd rather not. I'll save her feminine blushes. Please tell her from me that I wish her all the best in her choice of a marriage partner."

"Is that all?" asked Cliff, looking disappointed. "Aren't you going to..."

"Fight for her?" broke in Diba, half in jest. Cliff must have come prepared for a showdown. He could imagine him telling the girl not to worry, and that he would be able to fix Diba. His chance of showing himself a hero was slipping away.

"Er, well, if you loved her and..."

"For heaven's sake, Cliff, be sensible. I've only just met her. If she doesn't want to marry me, there are many other fish in the water." He meant that to hurt and the other looked offended and clenched his fist.

"You're a, a, ..." he said, shaking his fist at Diba.

"Keep cool," Diba advised. "What's biting you? That I wouldn't put up a fight for a woman? That I have handed her over to you on a golden plate? I can't see your problem."

Cliff looked a bit ashamed of himself. "Er, about the **bride price**, er, I'll repay every **kobo** as soon as..."

"That's between the families. Now, if you don't mind, I have lots of work to do. Good day and good luck."

Diba sat musing over the incident. He'd have to cancel the party he had organised to welcome his wife. No, he would not. A thought struck him and he began to laugh. The party would still go ahead but on the wall close to the bar he would hang a huge notice: **I've been jilted! Rejoice with me! Please enjoy yourselves!**

The party was well-attended and the guests enjoyed themselves. They did not believe that he had been jilted, anyway. So long as the music was good and there were lots to eat and drink, no one worried about why a party was being given.

Diba, who rarely took alcohol, decided to drown his disappointment in the stuff that night and the next morning he woke up with a gigantic **hangover**. He was glad it was a weekend and there was no important 'do' at the hotel. At mid-day he took some **aspirins** and felt a bit better. He took a book into the garden to read, but dozed off.

"Wake up Diba, wake up, please!" Someone was shaking him by the shoulder. The voice seemed to come from afar. It was **Ebi's**. He woke up and stretched, expecting the dream to clear away. It did not. Ebi was indeed before him, her face tear-stained. He rushed forward to take her in his arms, but stopped as she stood there wringing her hands, trying to control her sobs. His arms fell limply to his sides. It was uncanny, each time they met, she cried.

"What is it, Ebi?" he asked. "What are you doing in Port Harcourt?"

"It's er, Fa..., er, **Flint**. He's asking for you. Mother and Uncle **Tamu** are with him. They said you should please come at once."

Diba felt dizzy and began to tremble slightly at the news that his friend had escaped from jail. He pulled himself together.

"Oh, that's great," he said with false enthusiasm. "They are all in Port Harcourt, are they? When did they arrive?"

"We arrived five days ago, but Flint was brought here this morning."

"Was brought? Is he sick?"

"Yes, er, please you're to come at once, my father is dying, he's been shot by the police."

Ebi collapsed into a chair and began to weep uncontrollably. Diba was momentarily confused, then things began to fall into their places. **Father shot by the police?** Her father was dead, wasn't he? Who was this father? **Flint**, of course! How could he have been so stupid and blind? The resemblance was there in all the children. Flint, who had said that he was unmarried because he did not want his family to suffer for his crimes, was **Mrs. Oliga's husband** and the father of her children! He understood now the man's reluctance to send him to his family. He was touched that Flint had had to make such a sacrifice for him, and felt ashamed of himself for not wanting him out of jail.

Now Flint was wounded and on the run! Diba must go to him at once, and forget about getting involved. He must show himself a loyal friend.

"Come on, darling," he said, unaware of how naturally the word of endearment came to him. She looked at him with uncertainty as they stood face to face. She was trembling. He pulled her into his arms and kissed her.

"Diba," she said, brokenly, "what do you think of me now that you know who my father is?"

"In what way? I love you, Ebi. What your parents are doesn't matter."

"I mean, you know that er, Flint, my father, is of course the notorious **'Slippery Eel'**; the armed robber who has killed several people and is rated **Public Enemy No. 1**?"

"Sshh, don't distress yourself. If you must know, I like and respect him. He can't help what he is."

"I can't bring myself to hate him for what he is. My brothers and I have always loved him. It was as if by instinct we knew that he was our father. We were always happy whenever he was around. My mother loved him dearly too. I think he was the only man she ever loved."

"I think so too. That explains why she

never remarried."

"How did you become friends with Father? Did you know he was an armed robber?" Diba hesitated before he felt able to reply.

"Yes, I knew he was," he said slowly. So, Flint had not disclosed to his family where they had met. He was touched again by his friend's thoughtfulness. "We met under some funny circumstances. One day I'll tell you all about it." He would cook up a flippant story for the occasion. He did not think it was necessary to give her the exact details since Flint had not. The future would decide how the situation should be handled. Despite the shock he had received that day, he was in an elated mood at seeing his love again.

"Ebi," he said tenderly, taking her into his arms, "do you still love me? No, don't look away. I want to know the truth from your eyes."

"You know I can never stop loving you, Diba. I don't know how well you can read my eyes, but..."

"All right, that's enough for me, my precious. Will you marry me?"

"Yes, I'll marry you," she told him quietly.

"Even if your parents are against the match?"

"Even if they are against the match. I don't think Flint, er, Father would be against our marriage. He's very fond of you. Mother too." Suddenly she broke away from him and burst into tears.

"Oh, no, not again, darling," he teased, going after her. "What is it this time?"

"It's Father. He, he might be dead all this time I've been here talking to you."

"Oh, my God," cried Diba, becoming serious at once. "How selfish of me. We must set out at once. Come along."

On the way Ebi explained that she, her mother and Tamu had been in Port Harcourt for the **final burial ceremony** of her mother's aunt. Early that morning Flint had been brought in badly wounded in the chest. He had escaped from jail and had been on his way to Lagos, but he had been recognised by a policeman at a **check-point**. Instead of getting down from the vehicle, as he was requested to, he had opened fire on the police and had ordered his driver to drive on. The police had returned fire and he had been hit, but had escaped because the police had no vehicle to give them chase in.

When he had seen how critically wounded he was, he had asked the driver, who was a long-time acquaintance of his, to head straight for where his wife was in Port Harcourt. Mrs. Oliga had fainted when she saw the state of her husband. As no hospital would admit a patient with **gunshot wounds** without adequate explanations being given, and the police being informed, they had to call in a man who was an expert at **extracting bullets** to look after him. Although the man had tried his best, Ebi felt that her father must be taken to a good hospital where he could be properly looked

after. All the relatives were opposed to this
as they insisted that the incident must not
be made public. This was because they had
not believed Tamu's story about Flint being
shot by unknown persons while returning
from a late night party.

Flint was in very poor shape when they
got to the house but there was a weak smile
on his face as he recognised Diba, who could
not restrain his tears when he saw how
helpless and sick his daring friend was. He
sat by him and held his hand.

At about ten that night, Flint's condition
worsened and Ebi defied the elders by going
to phone for an **ambulance** to take him to
the hospital. It did not matter, she insisted,
if the police did get to know about the
incident. What was more important was
that Flint's life must be saved at all costs.
They would worry about other things later.

As they waited for the ambulance, Flint
beckoned to Diba and whispered in his ear.
Diba fought back tears as he looked around
wildly for help. Ebi rushed to her father's
side. His breaths were coming in great

gasps. Suddenly he sat up and began to cough up blood, then he gave one final convulsive heave, clutched his sides and fell back on the bed. He was dead. A loud wail rent the air and Mrs. Oliga fell down unconscious. Neither Ebi nor Diba had noticed her come into the room to witness the final departure of her husband.

Later Diba heard the full story from Mrs. Oliga. The man she had loved so much and who she had lost that morning had, many years before, defiantly admitted to her that he was **'Slippery Eel'**, the notorious armed robber who had been terrorising the southern parts of the country. She had confronted him with a photograph which had appeared in one of the **national dailies**. Despite the alias and the heavy disguise, she had recognised her husband. She had been astounded by his confession but, because of her devotion, she had begged him on her knees to give up his life of crime if not for her sake, at least for that of the children. He had laughed in that careless manner of his and had said that he would never live any other sort of life. No, not even if his parents came out of their graves and pleaded with him. Threats of leaving him and taking away the children did not move him. She felt she had lost him, and from that moment had considered herself a **widow**. They had parted, and penniless and in sorrow, she had gone back to her parents in Port Harcourt. She had refused to accept any financial support from him for herself and the children. She could not bring herself knowingly to accept the proceeds of armed robbery.

For a long time she had been enveloped in her grief, but had remained in love with him. It was agreed that he should keep away from the children for a while so that they could forget him as their father. Later, he turned up for visits as **'Uncle'**.

Flint was given a very quiet burial attended by about ten people only. He would have been very disappointed, thought Diba grimly as the wife and children were led away from the graveside, weeping. He would have preferred something more **flamboyant** with lots of music and merrymaking. He had lived his life the way he wanted to and had often told him in **Sabo Prison** that, when he died, he wanted no mourning by anyone to darken his path in the **life beyond** because he was sure to be **jiving** to **rock and roll** music as he went along to face his maker. Diba could not tell his family this, of course, and they had all turned up in black. He suspected that the five strange men who hovered in the background in the cemetery were **plain-clothes policemen**. However, no questions were asked and nothing appeared in the papers.

When her period of mourning was over, Mrs. Oliga married **Tamu** and they settled in Port Harcourt. No one was in the least surprised. He had always loved her although he had remained in the background all those years, lending a helping hand when necessary.

No man could ever replace Flint in **Caro Oliga's** heart but she knew that solid Tamu would provide her with all the solace she needed. One of her sons had taken over the management of the business and she was at last free to relax and enjoy what was left of her life.

"Now, isn't that sweet and civilised of him!" exclaimed Ebi as she opened one of her wedding gifts in a hotel room in **Enugu** where she and her husband were spending their **honeymoon**.

"Of whom, darling?" asked Diba, who was at the dressing table, mixing drinks from an array of bottles before him.

"Of **Princewill**, love," chuckled Ebi. "Look," she said, going over to Diba with a beautifully framed picture of her and Princewill, arm-in-arm, taken on a beach in Lagos a few years before. "He's given us this to hang over our bed, " he says. It's his wedding present for us." She collapsed with laughter. "He gave it to me as we were leaving."

"How dare he!" fumed Diba, pulling out the picture from its frame and tearing it up. He threw the lot into the dustbin. "The scoundrel!"

"Well," said Ebi, wiping her eyes, "he's entitled to his bit of fun. After all, you married his fiancée without his consent!"

"He doesn't exist as far as I am concerned." Diba went over to the window and held up a glass to the light.

"Is that right? Hey, what have you got in there? It looks absolutely wicked!"

"One of my concoctions." Diba smiled. "Tastes wicked too. Here, have a sip."

"Hm! I don't fancy it. It's too strong. It seems to knock my head off."

Diba laughed. "It's meant to. Customers will love it. The bar manager likes it very much and it's going to be a specialty of our restaurant."

"Great. What will you call it?"

"**Flinta-go-go**. It's named after the best friend I ever had. The only person who really cared about me." It was thought-provoking that the person who had helped him directly and indirectly to get reabsorbed and reintegrated into society was a man who was **enemy to that society**.

"What about me? Don't I care about you?"

"Well, yes, in your own way. But that's different. Come, my darling, let's drink to his memory."

They raised their glasses solemnly and drank.

www.ingramcontent.com/pod-product-compliance
Lightning Source LLC
Chambersburg PA
CBHW060418310726
48976CB00003B/1100